ON A TERRACE

"Rosalind," he murmured. "Rosie. You are so beautiful." One of his magical fingers trailed down her cheek, traced her lips.

She? Beautiful? She had never thought so before; she was too tall, too redheaded, too freckled. In his arms, at this moment, she was beautiful. He made it so.

"Not as beautiful as you, Lord Morley."

He smiled, and his hands slid up to cradle her face. "My name is Michael." The name was dark and sweet, like a cup of chocolate, a sip of brandy, in her mouth. "Michael."

He groaned, and bent his head to kiss her again. She fell back against the wall of the house. The stone was cold and sharp through the thick silk of her gown, but she scarely noticed it when Lord Morley— *Michael*—leaned in close to her. His lips slid from hers along the line of her throat, down to her bare shoulder.

"So sweet," he whispered, the words reverberating against her skin.

The Rules of Love

Amanda McCabe

A SIGNET BOOK

SIGNET
Published by New American Library, a division of
Penguin Group (USA) Inc., 375 Hudson Street,
New York, New York 10014, U.S.A.
Penguin Books Ltd, 80 Strand,
London WC2R 0RL, England
Penguin Books Australia Ltd, 250 Camberwell Road,
Camberwell, Victoria 3124, Australia
Penguin Books Canada Ltd, 10 Alcorn Avenue,
Toronto, Ontario, Canada M4V 3B2
Penguin Books (N.Z.) Ltd, Cnr Rosedale and Airborne Roads,
Albany, Auckland 1310, New Zealand

Penguin Books Ltd, Registered Offices:
80 Strand, London WC2R 0RL, England

First published by Signet, an imprint of New American Library,
a division of Penguin Group (USA) Inc.

First Printing, April 2004
10 9 8 7 6 5 4 3 2 1

Chapter One

"Family disagreements should be avoided if at all possible. If not possible, they should always take place in private, away from the eyes of servants and friends."
—*A Lady's Rules for Proper Behavior*, Chapter Two

"*O*h, Allen. What have you done *this* time?"

Though she'd spoken softly, Rosalind wanted to groan the words, scream them out, even throw something at her brother's head as he lounged so casually in his chair across from her. She could not, of course. That would be highly improper, and it would never do if one of the teachers or, heaven forbid, one of the girls heard her make a fuss. So she folded her hands on the mahogany surface of her desk, clasping her fingers together until the knuckles turned white.

Besides, even if she *did* throw something at Allen, it would scarcely make a dent in his thick skull. This was a scene they had played out dozens of times, and it always ended the same way.

"Oh, now, Rosie, really that is unfair," Allen protested. He crossed his booted foot over his buckskin-covered knee and jiggled it impatiently. Rosalind frowned as flakes of mud showered from the boot's sole onto the freshly polished floor. "I have done nothing untoward! A man must pay his gaming debts, after all. It is a point of honor."

Honor? Rosalind's head pounded as if a hundred

drummers were tattooing that word inside her brain. She should show him *honor*, the ignorant young pup!

Be calm, she thought, pressing her fingertips to her temples. *Remember how your parents asked you to look after him.*

Remember the rules. Breaking his skull was assuredly against the rules.

She reached out for the frighteningly official-looking letter. "So you borrowed money from a bank?"

"It was only until I receive my allowance. I needed to pay Carteret right away, you see, or I could not have shown my face at the club. They were never supposed to bother *you*, Rosie. It's dashed embarrassing to have them go to one's sister! What if Morley, or one of the others at the club, found out?"

Morley again. Always the blasted Viscount Morley. Even the very name made Rosalind silently curse, which usually she would never dream of doing. Cursing was also against the rules. Morley was the one who led Allen, and no doubt other impressionable young men, into folly. Morley, and his club, were a terrible influence on Allen.

But Rosalind did not say that. Any time she tried to talk to Allen about Lord Morley and his questionable activities, to warn him, he cut her off. It was futile— as futile as urging him to concentrate more on his studies and less on the lures of Town.

"Your allowance would never have covered this amount," she told him. "Not in a year. And the interest . . . !" Rosalind took a deep breath. "Allen, banks have ways of compelling people to pay. This is a legal debt. Do you have any idea what you have gotten yourself, not to mention this school and me, into?"

Allen's face, so bored and careless-looking ever since he had come into her office, flushed a dull red. His foot slid off his knee to land with a loud thud on the floor and he pointed a shaking finger in her direction. "Now, see here, Rosie! I am eighteen now. I can't stand for having my sister ring a peal over my head. I must live my own life, as a man."

Rosalind had had just about all she could take of this scene. Her head was pounding as if it would explode, and she knew that nothing she could say or do would persuade Allen of the truth. These days, only *Morley* could do that.

"I must remind you that I am your guardian until you are twenty, along with Uncle Silas, though truly I do everything since he lives in the wilds of Yorkshire. Our parents wished it this way, and in any case they left neither of us much money. It is *your sister* who pays for your schooling at Cambridge, as well as your allowance, and it is *your sister* who pulls you out of the soup every time you fall in. Which has been more and more of late!" Her voice rose dangerously on those last words. Rosalind took another deep breath and folded her hands together again. She would *not* let this get the better of her. "We are not wealthy people. This school allows us to be quite comfortable, but we cannot be extravagant as Mo—as some of your friends are."

Allen crossed his arms across his chest, still mulishly stubborn. "I am not *extravagant,* Rosie! I only need the necessities."

"Such as gaming debts? Coats from Weston? New boots every week?"

"I told you, it was the—"

Rosalind held up her hand to stop his endless flow of protests and explanations. "I know. It was for your club."

"Well—yes. It was. You must agree that a man must maintain his good name at his club."

Rosalind sighed, and resisted the almost overpowering urge to sink back wearily in her chair. She wished she could take a tisane and crawl into her bed, to sleep and forget all this. But she could not. It was too early in the day, and she had far too many responsibilities. The parents of her pupils would be arriving soon to take their daughters home for the spring holiday, for the beginning of the Season in London.

"I cannot think about this right now, Allen," she

said. "Most of the students are leaving today, and I must see them off."

Allen nodded, obviously deeply relieved. He never liked quarrels, even when he was the one who started them. "Of course, Rosie. I'll just come back tomorrow, then, or the day after."

Two days. That would give him plenty of time to run up even more debts, Rosalind thought. He would never learn. She just nodded, though, and watched him gather up his hat and greatcoat and hurry to the door.

There he turned back and gave her an uncertain glance, a flicker of a pleading smile. "Er, Rosie, about that letter from the bank . . ."

Rosalind stared down at the letter beneath her clenched hands. The stark black signature stared back, like an accusation. An accusation that she was failing in her duties to her family. Her parents, her flighty, social mother and her distracted vicar father, had always relied on her to look after Allen. Now that they were gone, she owed that to them even more. She was all Allen had. "I will write to them, and see what can be done. I will take care of it." *As always.*

Allen gave her a relieved smile, and came back to kiss her cheek. "You *are* a brick, Rosie. I knew you would see that it could not be helped."

She answered his grin with a stern frown. "I do not see any such thing. All I see is that banks must be dealt with. But I have no time to talk about this now. Just go, Allen."

Rosalind closed her eyes, and did not open them again until she heard the click of the door closing.

Alone at last. Her office, her sanctuary, looked the same as it always did. The lovely, restful lavender and cream draperies and chairs and settees, chosen to be feminine and soothing, were the same. The small mahogany desk she sat behind, the painting of pink and white roses that hung above the fireplace, the porcelain shepherdesses and vases on the tables—all the same. This room was where she could come to be alone, to be quiet, to do what she loved most in the world—write, and run her school.

Yet after such meetings with her brother, such futile, ridiculous meetings, nothing could soothe her.

"If only I wasn't a lady," she murmured, "I would have a whiskey."

Just as her late husband Charles had when things became too contentious. It had always soothed the few rough patches in their marriage.

But she *was* a lady. She had standards—high standards—to uphold. And the parents of her pupils would be arriving soon to fetch their precious daughters for their holidays. It would simply never do to greet them with *whiskey* on her breath!

She would have to content herself with a cup of tea in the drawing room, with those very parents.

Rosalind stood up and crossed the room to the small mirror hanging on the wall between two bookcases. She feared her reflection would show her inner turmoil, with wild eyes and straggling hair. Aside from a pink flush in her cheeks, however, she looked the same as she always did. Her bright red curls, the bane of her life, were drawn tightly back and covered with a lace cap. The frill of her chemisette was spotlessly white, tucked neatly into the square neckline of her green and gold striped silk afternoon dress. Her blue eyes *were* brighter than usual, sparkling with the force of suppressed anger, but other than that she was the perfectly proper Mrs. Chase.

She opened the little hidden drawer in one of the bookcases and took out a small pot of rice powder and one of lip color. She dusted the powder over the faint golden freckles that splashed across the bridge of her nose. Not for the first time, she wished she had Allen's smooth chestnut locks and clear complexion, instead of the red hair and freckles that came from their grandmother.

The thought of her brother made her eyes narrow again, and pink spread across her cheeks and down her throat into the ruffle.

"Not now," she murmured. "I cannot think of this now. Allen will just have to stew in his own soup for the moment."

There was a knock at the door. It was probably Molly, the housemaid, come to tell her that the first of the parents were arriving. Rosalind pushed the powder and lip color back into the drawer, and called, "Come in."

It was not Molly's face that peeked around the door, though. It was Lady Violet Bronston.

Rosalind couldn't help but smile at the sight of Lady Violet's golden curls and merry green eyes. She was one of the best students at Mrs. Chase's Seminary for Young Ladies, adept at music, watercolors, and French. She was sweet, and friendly with the other girls, a great favorite of the teachers. And of Rosalind, too, if truth be told. Violet's conversation was always cheerful, despite the fact that her family life was not entirely happy. Rosalind would miss her when she graduated and went on to her first Season next year.

Yes, Violet *was* a dear. Even if she was the sister of Viscount Morley.

"I am sorry to disturb you, Mrs. Chase," Violet said shyly. She glanced around quickly. Usually only Rosalind and the teachers came into this office.

Rosalind smiled at her, and gestured for her to enter. "Please, do come in, Lady Violet. You are not disturbing me at all. I was just going to come and be sure that everyone is packed. Is your father here to fetch you already?" She said this most pleasantly, even though her lips wanted to twist bitterly at mention of Violet's father. The Earl of Athley was certainly an important man indeed, but also a most unpleasant and arrogant one. He was assuredly one of the most difficult of the parents to deal with. Fortunately, she seldom saw him.

Rosalind also thought Lord Athley could use a thorough lesson in manners.

Violet shook her head, a relieved smile on her rosebud lips. "No, indeed! Papa could not come today.

My brother, Lord Morley, is going to fetch me and take me into Town."

Morley again. Could not an hour pass that she did not hear that name? Rosalind covered her chagrin by turning away to pick up her shawl and drape it over her shoulders. "Your brother? We have not seen him here in quite a while." Not since that one disastrous visit last year. That had not gone well at all.

Violet sat down on one of the brocade settees, happily oblivious to any possible strife in her small world. She smoothed the skirt of her stylish, pale lilac carriage gown. "He came to see me last month, when you had gone to Bath. He says he will take me to have ices at Gunter's when we are in London, and to the theater, and Astley's Amphitheater, so that—well, so that I do not have to spend *all* my time with Father at Bronston House."

Rosalind sat down beside Violet, surprised to hear of such generosity from such an annoying man. "That sounds lovely for you."

Violet nodded, and stared down at her lace-gloved hands folded in her lap. "Yes, of course. But I *will* miss the school so much! And you, and Miss James, and the other girls. I wish . . ." She paused and swallowed hard before she went on in a softer voice. "I wish I could stay here."

Rosalind nodded. She had had this discussion with Violet before, had listened to the girl when she spoke of her unhappiness at home. It made Rosalind's heart ache that she could do so little for her. "Some of the girls *do* stay here for the holidays, of course," she said carefully. "But most of them have family homes that are far away, not nearby as yours is."

Violet nodded. "I know, and Father would never hear of my staying here." She gave Rosalind a brave, bright little smile, and said, "But I promise you, Mrs. Chase, that my time in London will not be wasted! I will work on my watercolors, and my French verbs. And Miss James has assigned us to read *Hamlet*, which is very good since my brother has promised to take

me to see the play at Drury Lane." She opened her
reticule and pulled out a small book, handsomely
bound in dark blue leather. The embossed silver letters on the cover read *A Lady's Rules for Proper Behavior*. "And I will always be very careful to follow
the rules. A true lady is known by her manners, is she
not? That is what you always say, Mrs. Chase."

Rosalind laughed. "Yes, of course. And a true gentleman, too. Manners are what raise us above the ani-
mals in their forests and barnyards. They are the mark
of true civility."

Violet nodded eagerly. "I read it every night." She
ran her fingertip over the silver words, *By an Anonymous Lady*. "Do you think we shall ever know who
wrote it?"

"Perhaps not. But that is not important, Lady Violet. What *is* important is the content of its pages."

Violet tucked the book carefully back into her reticule. "Perhaps I should get a copy for my brother?"

*I doubt it would do him much good, he is so far
gone,* Rosalind thought wryly. But outwardly she just
nodded, and said, "I am sure Lord Morley would appreciate that. Now, my dear Lady Violet, tell me what
else you have planned for your holiday."

She half-listened as Violet talked of tea parties and
museums. Yet in her mind she saw the most dis-
tracting image of *A Lady's Rules* in the philistine
hands of Lord Morley.

For Rosalind had a secret, an even greater one than
the rice powder that covered her freckles. She herself
was the anonymous lady who wrote the very popular
Rules. And the sales of this slim volume, so dependent
on its interest among the *ton*, helped pay her own,
and her brother's, bills. Fortunately for her, Lord Morley and his ilk were in the minority in Society at the
moment. *A Lady's Rules* had become all the crack
among the *haute ton*. Everyone was eager to buy the
book and show how very civilized they were.

That tiny book was Rosalind's very life's blood.

Chapter Two

"Young ladies are particularly impressionable,
and look to their families for a fine example.
Proper behavior and language, while always
important, should be especially observed in
their presence"
—*A Lady's Rules for Proper Behavior*, Chapter One

*M*ichael Bronston, the Viscount Morley, drew his
phaeton to a halt on the gravel drive outside
Mrs. Chase's Seminary for Young Ladies, and sat
there for a moment, studying the surroundings. The
Seminary was only a few miles outside London, but it
might as well have been on another continent, so different was it from the rush and noise of the city. Situ-
ated in its own green, tidy park, surrounded by a high
wall, it had almost the hush of a monastery.

The school building itself was of red brick, faded by
time to a rose pink, with neat white shutters at the
windows and white pillars lining the portico. Heavy
draperies hung inside all the windows, shutting out
the light.

Michael frowned at its terribly tidy, terribly proper
appearance.

A fitting prison for my poor sister, he thought. Then
he had to laugh at himself. It seemed the whole "poet
persona" he took on himself in Society was beginning
to tell on him. He was becoming melodramatic.

And, prison though the Seminary might be for Vio-

let, it was far better for her than being at home. Their
father was a more accomplished jailer than Mrs. Chase
could ever hope to be.

Ah, yes. *Mrs. Chase.* The beauteous Mrs. Chase,
who tried to hide her glorious sunset-colored hair
under hideous caps, and whose disapproving moue
made her seem far older than she surely was. Michael
had met her only once, on one of the occasions he
came to visit Violet, but her cool glance had almost
frozen him where he stood.

There was something *about* her, though, something
in the pale depths of her ice blue eyes that made him
want to bait her, to tweak her maddening propriety—
to make her show some emotion. So he, perhaps child-
ishly, had acted even more the "poet" around her,
lounging indolently in the dainty chairs of her drawing
room, quoting suggestive verse to her.

Mrs. Chase had merely raised her chin even higher,
and stared at him as if he was an insect on her polished floor. And Violet had berated him for his lack
of manners for hours afterward. It had not been his
proudest moment. He had been deeply relieved to find
Mrs. Chase gone to Bath on his next visit to Violet.

But now here he was again, and there was very little
hope that Mrs. Chase would not be on the premises.
He vowed that this time he would act his age, and be
impeccably well-mannered. He had even brought a
sort of peace offering, a volume of his newest collection of poems, though he doubted it would thaw any
of Mrs. Chase's frostiness.

A footman in the school livery came to take the
reins of the phaeton, and Michael jumped down to
the gravel drive. No sooner had he placed one booted
foot on the front steps than the white-painted door
opened and Mr. Allen Lucas came barreling out.

The young man was scowling, distracted, until he
saw Michael, and a grin lit up his face.

"Lord Morley!" he cried happily, and caught Michael's hand in a hearty shake. "Fancy meeting you
here, of all places."

Michael remembered then that Lucas was Mrs. Chase's brother. It was hard to remember that when he saw the young man at their club every week; his behavior and demeanor were so very different from hers. Allen Lucas was one of a group of young men, newcomers to the Thoth Club, who had literary and artistic pretensions and who spent most of their time trying to outdo one another in hell-raising.

"I've come to fetch my sister home," Michael said, pulling off his leather driving gloves.

Lucas gave a lopsided grin, which he obviously considered sardonic, and leaned against one of the pillars. "And I've just left *my* sister."

"Your sister is Mrs. Chase, is she not?"

"The very same." Lucas heaved a deep sigh, full of exasperation. "I vow I will never be able to fathom females! Rosie has become such a dry stick, and I don't know when it happened. She was always laughing, always game for a lark, when we lived at my parents' house."

Mrs. Chase, of the icy blue eyes and tilted chin, game for a lark? Mrs. Chase, called *Rosie*? Somehow, Michael could not envision it. But then, he very often could not fathom females, either. "So you are leaving, Lucas?"

"Indeed, and the quicker the better, before Rosie finds me and rings another peal over my head. See you at the club on Thursday? I heard Lord Waverly and Mr. Gilmore are going to race their curricles!"

"Not in the club, I do hope."

Lucas guffawed loudly, far more loudly than the light jest deserved. "Certainly not! The road to Brighton, I daresay. But it will be on the betting books."

"Ah. Well, then, I will see you there. Good day, Lucas."

"Good day, Morley!" Lucas bounded down the steps to where a footman held the reins of his horse.

Morley gave him a farewell wave, and then turned back to the front door. Lucas had left it ajar on his exit, so Michael just pushed it open and went in.

The foyer was crowded with piles of trunks and valises, with girls in fluttery pastel travel gowns, who called to each other, and giggled, and cried as they tied their bonnet ribbons and draped shawls over their shoulders. Footmen and teachers moved between them, carrying bags away or just shifting them about. Michael glanced back to the door he had just entered. It seemed to be a portal back to sanity, out of bedlam.

But he was too late. Miss James, one of the teachers, saw him before he could make his escape.

"Lord Morley!" she called. She handed one of the girls a pink bandbox and made her way over to him, wending past the obstacles of luggage. "How good it is to see you again. Lady Violet has been asking every five minutes when you would arrive."

"Hello, Miss James," Michael answered. He pushed away his doubts about all the feminine fuss, and gave her a polite bow. "I must say I am quite eager to see my sister again, too. It has been far too long."

"Such brotherly devotion is most touching, Lord Morley." Miss James smiled at him rather mistily. "Lady Violet is in the drawing room. Mrs. Chase is serving tea in there, as well. I am sure you must be in need of refreshment after your long drive."

"Thank you, Miss James." Michael bowed to her again, and made his way toward the door that led to the drawing room, trying not to knock over any scurrying young misses or fall over any errant trunks on the way.

It was slightly quieter in the elegant pale green and cream drawing room. There was no luggage piled about, only the usual chairs and tables and bibelots. Parents, and a few daughters, gathered in clusters and groups, chatting and laughing in perfectly civilized tones. On one large, round table was an array of tea things—cups, pots, tiered trays of tiny sandwiches and cakes.

There was a small, barely perceptible lull in the conversation when Michael appeared, and a few female glances turned his way. He was not entirely thrilled to meet the dark gaze of Lady Clarke. They had flirted casually at a ball or two, but she had soon spread the word that Michael's poem, "Alas, fair cruelty," was about *her*. It most decidedly was not. She gave him a little wave of her dainty fingers.

Michael acknowledged her greeting with a brief nod, but his own gaze was caught by the woman who stood next to the tea table—Mrs. Chase. She had not seen him yet, and was talking to one of the parents. She nodded at whatever the other woman was saying, and tilted her head thoughtfully to one side. Her hair was smoothed back beneath an ugly lace cap, but one flame red curl had fallen from its confines and tangled with a pearl drop earring. She reached up absently to brush it back, and the curl twined around her slender finger before she managed to confine it.

Then, unexpectedly, she laughed. Really laughed. The sound reached all the way across the room to him, wrapping around him silkily, as her hair had caught on her finger. It was sweet and rich, surprisingly dark, like a Spanish sherry. It transformed her entire being, making her face, usually so pale and distant, glow with an incandescent radiance.

"Aurora, the dawn . . ." he whispered.

As if she heard him, though that was impossible from across the room, she looked up and saw him standing there. The laughter faded as if it had never been. Her eyes turned from sky blue to ice, and her lips thinned.

Michael wanted her laughter back—more than wanted, he *needed* it. He could not have said why he mourned the loss of this woman's merriment. She was a person he hardly knew, did not even *like*. But there it was. He found he would do anything to hear her laugh again.

As if in some sort of a trance, a daze, he took a step toward her, then another.

The invisible cord that pulled him to Mrs. Chase snapped when he heard his sister's silvery voice call, "Michael! Here you are at last."

Michael blinked, as if awakening from some dream, and rubbed his hand roughly over his eyes. That—that *whatever* it was that had come over him dissipated, and he found himself still in the school drawing room. He glanced quickly over to where Mrs. Chase had gone back to her conversation, half turned away from him. She was hardly an Aurora; she was just a stern schoolmistress.

"I am sorry I was delayed, Vi," he said, catching his sister's hands in his and leaning down to kiss her dimpled cheek. "There was a great deal of traffic on the road from London. It was all coming here, I see."

"Oh, yes, indeed! It is always crowded before holidays." Violet smiled up at him, those dimples flashing. "It is very good to see you again, Michael."

"And it's good to see *you*, Vi. It has been far too long." His sister was looking very well, he thought, as he held her away from him so he could study her. She had always been a pretty girl, the very image of their late mother with her golden curls and grass green eyes. But she had always been rather quiet, too, lost in her own world. Here, away from their father, she seemed more confident, more a part of the world around her.

If only she would learn to follow her own way in that world, and not follow in the paths of others so much.

"Oh, Vi!" he teased. "When did my baby sister grow to be such a grand lady?" He caught her up in a hug, until her little feet left the floor.

"Michael!" she squealed, pushing him away. "There are people watching."

He laughed. "So, since people are watching, I am not allowed to greet my sister?"

Violet frowned up at him, her pink and white forehead puckering, her lips drawn together in a perfect imitation of Mrs. Chase. She opened the reticule that dangled from her wrist and drew out a small, blue leather-bound book. She flicked through the pages until she found what she was looking for, and she read aloud, "'A gentleman shall never be overexuberant when greeting a lady, even one nearly related to him. Bowing over the hand, or, if closely related, a kiss on the cheek, will suffice.' "

Michael laughed again, thinking she could not be serious. But Violet's frown deepened, and she even tapped the toe of her kid half-boot against the floor.

"Michael!" she scolded. "The rules are not to be mocked. They are important. Manners are what make us *civilized*."

"What on earth are you spouting about, Vi?" Michael asked, and grabbed the book out of her hands.

A Lady's Rules for Proper Behavior.

Michael almost groaned aloud. So the insidious "rules" had spread out from Town into the Seminary. And his own sister was an adherent.

He should have known that Mrs. Chase, of all people, would read and espouse this book.

Violet took the volume back, and tucked it into her reticule. "You should read it, Michael. It is really most edifying."

"Edifying, eh?" Michael couldn't resist reaching out to tweak one of his sister's sunshine curls. "They *do* teach you big words here."

Violet drew back with another frown. "You see, Michael? You *do* need to read the rules. A gentleman should never pull a lady's hair. But come and say hello to Mrs. Chase now! I have told her all about our plans for the holiday."

"Did you, indeed?" he muttered. He politely offered Violet his arm, and led her across the room toward Mrs. Chase. He pasted an amiable smile on his lips, but inwardly he hoped he could just keep himself from throttling Mrs. Chase. She was turning his sweet sister into a rule-following stick—just like their father.

Chapter Three

> "A gentleman must never seat himself on the settee beside his hostess, or any lady not related to him, unless invited."
> —*A Lady's Rules for Proper Behavior,* Chapter Five

*R*osalind watched Lord Morley's exuberant greeting of his sister—and almost laughed when Lady Violet pulled out *A Lady's Rules* and proceeded to read her brother a portion of it. She did not know which rule it could be, but it must be a good one to cause the dark frown on Lord Morley's face. He stepped back from Violet, his hands planted on his hips, leather driving gloves dangling carelessly from his curled fingers.

Lady Violet, usually the mildest of young ladies, looked like a fierce little Valkyrie, swooping down to avenge wrongs done to decorum.

Rosalind thought again what a very fine student Lady Violet was.

"Ah, I see Lord Morley is here!" said the woman Rosalind was talking to, Lady Stone-Smythe. She reached up to pinch some color into her plump cheeks, and straightened her pink and green confection of a bonnet. "Such a treat to get a glimpse of him. He is invited simply *everywhere,* you know, but is so unpredictable in which invitations he will accept. I have hopes he will come to the literary evening I have planned." She half-turned toward where Lord Morley

stood, displaying her ample charms in a tight green
carriage costume to better advantage. "Imagine seeing
him at a ladies' seminary."

Rosalind thought of one or two rules Lady Stone-
Smythe would be well-advised to follow, but she resisted the urge to say so. Lady Stone-Smythe had three
daughters in the school, and was one of her finest
patrons. Even if she *was* a bit of silly goose.

"Lord Morley is the brother of one of my pupils,
Lady Violet Bronston," Rosalind said. "She told me
he was going to escort her home today."

"Of course! Lady Violet. Such a lovely young lady.
And she is such good friends with my Imogen. I must
go and say hello to her." With nary another glance
at Rosalind, Lady Stone-Smythe sailed off across the
drawing room to greet Lady Violet, clutching at the
young woman's hand with great enthusiasm.

Violet stared at her, obviously bewildered, while her
brother looked on, one corner of his lips lifted in
amusement. Rosalind realized with a start that those
lips were really quite handsome, narrow but sensual.
She shook her head hard. What was she doing, thinking of his *handsome* lips! Ridiculous.

When Lady Stone-Smythe turned her effusions onto
him, the quirk became a charming smile, and he
bowed over her outstretched hand in its bright pink
glove.

Rosalind could not fault his performance. His expression was interested, but not *too* interested, as he
listened to Lady Stone-Smythe, leaning slightly closer
as if to better hear her words.

Lady Stone-Smythe's performance, on the other
hand . . .

Rosalind sighed, and poured a bit more tea in her
cup. Some people, no matter how often they read the
rules, simply never learned.

"Mrs. Chase," a voice said, interrupting her musings
on Lord Morley, Lady Stone-Smythe, and proper
behavior.

Rosalind turned to see Lady Clarke walking toward

her, her daughter Emmeline in tow. Lady Clarke was one of the reigning Diamonds of the *ton,* tall, willowy, with dark, glossy hair and perfect snow-white skin, set off elegantly by her dark red pelisse and tall-crowned hat. Sir Walter Clarke, whom Rosalind had met only once and who was not present today, was also quite handsome, a perfect match for his wife. Rosalind wondered what *he* would think of his wife's attention to the poet.

For Lady Clarke's gaze, like that of Lady Stone-Smythe, slid irresistibly to one magnetic object—Lord Morley.

Lady Clarke smiled charmingly at Rosalind, but kept sending tiny, surreptitious glances across the room. "Mrs. Chase, it is time Emmeline and I were leaving for Town, but we could not go without saying good-bye to you first. Emmeline has so enjoyed her time here, and is looking forward to returning next term."

Rosalind turned to Emmeline, who was a tall, dark girl, not yet revealing any beauty she might have inherited. "I am so glad you have enjoyed your time here, Emmeline. You have certainly been a fine addition to the school."

Emmeline murmured something and dropped a quick curtsy before hurrying off to join some of her friends.

"Your daughter is very talented musically, Lady Clarke," Rosalind told Emmeline's mother. "Her performances at the pianoforte are very pleasing."

"Oh, yes? How—very nice," Lady Clarke answered, without much interest. She still stared across the room, and reached up to finger the stiff lace trim of her pelisse. "I see that Lord Morley is here. Imagine encountering him at a girls' school."

Her words were almost exactly what Lady Stone-Smythe's had been, and Rosalind gave her the same answer. Lord Morley was here to fetch his sister.

"Indeed?" Lady Clarke said. Her touch moved from the lace to the ruby drop in her earlobe. "I—that is,

we see him quite often in Town. We do try to support
literature and music, and he is such a fine—poet. Have
you read his work, Mrs. Chase?"

"No," Rosalind answered. "I have not had the
privilege."

"Oh, you really should. A lady with a school should
always be au courant, don't you agree? Well-versed
in poetry and such."

"Indeed yes, Lady Clarke," Rosalind answered
stiffly. "A girl cannot truly call herself a lady until she
has attained accomplishments such as music, lan-
guages, and proper demeanor." Chapter One, *A
Lady's Rules for Proper Behavior.*

Lady Clarke gave her one final, dismissive nod, and
moved on to find her daughter. Before she reached
Emmeline, though, she took a small detour to Lord
Morley's side. As Rosalind watched, Lady Clarke laid
an elegant hand on his sleeve, and said something quietly into his ear. He grinned at her, and she gave
his arm a tiny, nearly imperceptible squeeze before
moving away.

Oh, really, Rosalind thought wryly. Her school was
not a place of assignation for Lord Morley! It was not
a *harem.*

She turned away to place her empty cup back on
the table. As she did so, she remembered that she had
a small gift for Lady Violet in her office, and she
should fetch it before the Bronstons left. She excused
herself to the parents and teachers around her and
left the drawing room.

Her office was quiet and peaceful after the milling
throng of people, the early afternoon light a pale gold
where it fell from the high windows. Rosalind fetched
the little package from her desk drawer, but then,
rather than return immediately to the drawing room,
she sat down in her chair. Her earlier headache was
still there, lurking behind her eyes, and she rubbed at
her temples and closed her eyes.

She loved the girls who went to school here; she
loved teaching. But she was also so glad when they

all left for their holidays, and she had days and nights of perfect quiet all for herself. It was—peaceful.

Peaceful, except for worrying about Allen.

She groaned at the reminder of Allen and his debt, and a new pain stabbed above her left eye.

"Mrs. Chase?" someone said. A *masculine* someone.

Rosalind pressed hard one more time at her temples, before she dropped her hands and opened her eyes, a polite smile automatically forming on her lips.

The smile died before it had even truly been born when she saw the man that voice belonged to. Lord Morley stood in the doorway, watching her with a concerned frown.

"Lord Morley," she said, lacing her fingers together atop the desk.

"Mrs. Chase, are you quite all right?" he asked, moving farther into the room. He stopped in the middle of her lavender and cream carpet, and glanced about almost as if he was surprised to find himself there. He totally ignored the mess of dried mud Allen had left behind. "You look pale."

Rosalind stared at him, her voice frozen in her throat. He seemed a mirage here in her frilly, feminine sanctuary. He was tall and dark, overpowering the dainty gilded furniture, his deep blue greatcoat spreading like the wings of some bird of prey.

He *was* handsome, she had to admit, even if he was a blackguard. Worthy of the stares and simpers of Lady Clarke and Lady Stone-Smythe—worthy in a physical sense, anyway. He was tall, slim but not emaciated. Lean, in the way horsemen and swimmers were. His black, curling hair, overlong in the poetical tradition, was brushed back from his forehead and tumbled over the collar of his coat. His nose was a bit crooked, as if it had once been broken, but his jaw was firm, and his eyes—his eyes were dark as a starless night, dark as sin.

Rosalind almost groaned, and she closed her eyes again. What was wrong with her? She had drunk no spirits today at all, yet she was staring like a wide-eyed, moonstruck schoolgirl. Staring at the man who was leading her brother to perdition! Was there a rule against this? She was too tired to recall for certain, but if there was not there *should* be. *A lady will not stare at the rogue who is intent on ruining the prospects of silly young men.*

She opened her eyes and stared down at her hands.

She realized she had not said anything for too long when he took another step toward her and said, with mounting alarm in his voice, "Mrs. Chase! Do you feel faint?"

"I am quite well, thank you, Lord Morley," she managed to say. She reached up to make certain her cap was firmly in place.

"Nonsense! You are as white as milk. I will be right back."

Rosalind opened her mouth to protest, but Lord Morley had already spun around on his heel and left the room.

Oh, now where had he gone? Rosalind stood up, bewildered and even a bit frightened. This situation was spinning beyond her control, and she did not even know how it had happened.

And if there was one thing Rosalind *hated,* it was not being in control of every situation. Before she could stumble to the door, though, Lord Morley returned, a cup of tea in his hand. The fragile, pink-flowered china looked tiny and absurd in his long, elegant fingers.

"Here," he said. "You should sit down, and drink this." With his free hand, he clasped her arm and led her to the nearest settee.

"It is nothing, Lord Morley," she protested, and tried to draw away from his strangely disturbing touch. He was too strong for her, though, and did not let go until she was safely seated. "A mere headache."

"It is no wonder your head aches," he said. "Listening to those clucking women all morning is enough to give anyone the megrims!" He handed her the cup of tea, and went on in a perfect imitation of Lady Stone-Smythe's fluting tones. " 'Oh, Mrs. Chase, my dear Harriet is *so* fond of playing the harp! You *must* allow her more time with the music master, she is *so* fond of him—I mean, fond of *music*.' "

Rosalind nearly choked on the sip of tea she had just taken. She knew she should not laugh at him, not find him funny in the least—it would only encourage his outrageous behavior, and it was surely rude to poor Lady Stone-Smythe. Yet she could not seem to help herself. She pressed her fingers to her lips to hold in the inelegant giggles.

"You see? Your color is better already, Mrs. Chase," he said, and knelt down beside her. He grinned in an infuriatingly satisfied manner.

"None of Lady Stone-Smythe's daughters is named Harriet," was all Rosalind could think to say.

"Ah, but you knew it was meant to be Lady Stone-Smythe. It must have been a worthy effort on my part."

"Yes, indeed, Lord Morley," Rosalind said tartly. Her dizziness was subsiding, and she felt a bit more like herself. Not like a woman who stared at rakes, thinking how handsome they were. "You ought to be treading the boards."

"So I think, but my family would simply not hear of it. I must content myself with poetry."

"Yes, your poetry." Rosalind swallowed the last of her tea, grateful for the strength of the smoky brew even if it was a bit cold by now. "Did Lady Stone-Smythe manage to lure you to her little literary evening?"

"She has been trying to for at least a month." As he shook his head in exasperation, his black raven's wing of hair fell over his brow, and he impatiently pushed it back.

Rosalind stared down at him, kneeling there on one knee beside her. "It is most improper for you to be there on the floor, Lord Morley," she said, yet there was not as much heat in the words as she would usually have put there. For once, she did not feel like scolding on a point of etiquette. She *did* want to touch that wave of hair, to see if it was as satiny as it appeared.

She curled her fingers tightly around the cup, and said, "It is not proper for you to be in here at all."

"You were ill, Mrs. Chase. Would it have been proper for me to leave you alone with your pain?"

"You could have fetched one of the teachers."

"They were all conversing with the parents of your pupils. I thought it best not to interrupt them."

Rosalind suspected that perhaps he had just not wanted all the ladies in his harem snatching at his sleeves again.

Her lips tightened at the thought.

Lord Morley moved up off the floor, but only to sit beside her on the settee. Rosalind, shocked by the sudden movement, slid back as far as she could against the arm of the settee. His heat still reached out to her, curling around her, beckoning her closer.

She turned away from it, away from *him,* pulling her skirts to the side so they would not brush against his boots. This was the man who was encouraging Allen in his wild ways, she reminded herself. This was not a man to be friends with, to sit close to. "Why were you in my office in the first place, Lord Morley? Was there something you wanted?"

His gaze slanted toward her, dark, surprisingly intense. "Wanted, Mrs. Chase? I suppose you could say that."

He said it as if—as if— She had not meant it in *that* way! Really, this man was maddening, twisting a simple word about until she hardly knew *what* she had been thinking. "Was it something concerning Lady Violet?"

The mention of his sister seemed to recall Lord Morley back to himself. He looked away from her. "Violet. Yes. She seems to like it here very much."

"I hope she does. We like *her* very much. She is one of our best students."

"Thank you, Mrs. Chase. I wanted to see you before I left today, to tell you how much I appreciate your kindness to Violet. I brought this for you, as a small gesture of thanks."

From inside his greatcoat, Lord Morley withdrew a small, tissue-wrapped package.

"A—a gift, Lord Morley?" Rosalind said, eyeing the harmless-looking package almost as if it could reach out and bite her. "I am not sure I should accept it."

"Really?" He raised his brow at her inquiringly, turning the tissue invitingly in his hand. "It is not a great deal, Mrs. Chase, surely not improper. It is for your library here."

Rosalind's curiosity got the better of her. She took the package from him, careful not to touch his fingers as she did so, and folded the tissue back. It was a book, bound in brown leather, decorated with gold gilt designs and lettering. She opened the cover to read the title page.

Songs to Athene, by Michael Bronston.

"Your—your poems, Lord Morley," she said. She did not know what she had been expecting. Rubies? Silken scarves? Though this was almost as disconcerting as those would have been.

"Violet tells me that you enjoy poetry," he said. He sounded a bit uncertain at her reaction.

"Yes, of course." She *did* enjoy poetry—Shakespeare, Donne, Spenser. The newfangled romantic, wild poetry of the sort Lord Morley wrote, it—well, it *disturbed* her.

But it was kind of him to bring it for their library, even if it was not the sort of thing the girls ought to be reading. She should give him something in return.

And there was only one thing she could think of that he needed. Needed in a most dire way.

She stood up and crossed the office to one of her bookcases, and extracted a volume from the shelf. Lord Morley had also stood, and followed her.

She held out the book. "Thank you for your gift,

Lord Morley," she said. "I would like to give you this in return."

"A *gift*, Mrs. Chase? I am shocked." He smiled at her, with that quirk at the corner of his lips. Then he looked down at the book—and the smile faded. *"A Lady's Rules for Proper Behavior."*

"Oh, yes," Rosalind answered firmly. She *did* feel more like herself, more like sensible, practical, proper Rosalind Lucas Chase. The strange spell Lord Morley had cast over her had obviously been a fleeting thing, brought about by their solitude in the office and her headache. "It is the one book that no one should be without. I believe that you in particular are most in need of it, Lord Morley."

Chapter Four

"The only proper gifts between unmarried ladies and gentlemen are flowers, sweets, or small books."
—*A Lady's Rules for Proper Behavior*, Chapter Seven

A Lady's Rules for Proper Behavior. She had given him a blasted book of etiquette!

Michael still could not cease thinking of it, even as he drove the phaeton out the Seminary gates and turned down the road toward London. Fortunately, Violet, on the seat beside him, was too preoccupied in studying the small silver locket Mrs. Chase had given her to notice his silence.

It was not so much that Mrs. Chase had given him the book, Michael thought. After all, she was a schoolmistress and would naturally advocate proper behavior, even of the extreme sort promulgated in that book. It was that she implied he was so greatly in need of it. What was it she had said? Oh, yes. "I believe that you in particular are most in need of it, Lord Morley."

As if he was an ape of some sort! A bumbling monkey with no idea of how to behave in a proper home.

It was true, he grudgingly admitted, that on his first visit to the Seminary he had not been all he should have been. He had needled Mrs. Chase and her deep propriety. He had spent his entire adult life striving against just such rigid mores, such shallow emphasis on conduct. And her stiff attitude had near driven him mad.

But he was sorry for his previous behavior, his boorishness. Had he not apologized to her, tried to make up for it? It was Mrs. Chase's home, and her guests had a duty to behave according to her—he winced to think the word—her *rules*. And he had mended his ways today, striving to behave within proper gentlemanly boundaries. Aside from his exuberant greeting of Violet, he had been everything that was proper. Even the Anonymous Lady who wrote *A Lady's Rules* would have approved of him. He had even given Mrs. Chase a book of his poetry!

What more could the woman want of him? What could ever erase the pinch of disapproval from her pretty—*too* pretty—lips?

And why was he thinking of her as pretty, anyway? Her caps were an absolute fright, and her eyes were frozen. There was nothing behind that ice blue façade—nothing but manners.

"Michael, why on earth are you driving so fast?" Violet cried, her voice edged with alarm.

Only then did Michael realize the great speed he had urged his horses to. They practically barreled along the road, dashing past the other now-gawking travelers into Town. The wheels clacked and whirred as if he was in a race.

He immediately drew back on the reins, slowing to a more moderate pace. "Sorry, Vi," he said, and threw his sister an apologetic smile.

She stared at him with wide, wary eyes. "Whatever were you thinking of? You looked a million miles away."

He sought quickly for a believable answer—anything but the truth. He could hardly tell her that he was thinking her teacher was a priss. "I was wondering which waistcoat I should wear to Lady Clarke's rout on Friday."

"Hmph." Violet folded her hands daintily in her lap, her mouth pursed. Michael saw that she had fastened the locket about her neck, the silver oval lying against the lace frill of her collar. He wondered if the gift from Mrs. Chase had somehow magically imparted some of that lady's qualities into his sister. "I think you should keep your thoughts on the road when you are driving."

Michael just laughed at her prim attitude, and reached out to tweak one of her curls again. He had often done that when she was a child, and it had always made her giggle.

Now she pushed him away, and said, "I also think you should keep both hands on the reins. Your horses look most unpredictable."

"Yes, Your Highness," Michael answered, in a mock-obsequious tone, and returned his gaze again to the road. When had his giggling sister turned into an elderly duchess? "But I would have you know that Nicodemus and Beelzebub are perfectly well-trained, and as gentle as lambs."

"Of course they are, with names like that." Violet turned her head away to study the passing landscape, so that all he could see of her was the brim of her white straw bonnet.

Silenced, he too watched their surroundings. The green expanses of the countryside were giving way to the edges of London. The grass was sparse, turning to pavement and gravel, the trees more stunted, the air heavier. The peace of the Seminary's grounds seemed a different world than that of the shouts and calls of the people—farmers going to market with their carts, racing aristocrats, workers on foot. On the road, they had been a trickle—now they became a flood. Michael had to slow the horses even further as they turned toward the rarefied air of Mayfair.

"I wish it did not take such a short time to get here," Violet murmured, so softly that Michael almost could not hear her. "I wish it took days and days. I wish the Seminary was in Scotland, or—or America."

She looked at Michael, and he saw that her eyes were misty with unshed tears. The prim duchess was again just a scared young girl.

"I know," he said, hating the damnable helpless feeling in his heart. "But it will not be so bad, I promise. You will be back at school next month, and in the meantime there are many things we can do."

She swiped her gloved hand over her eyes. "Gunter's, and the theater?"

"Of course. And I am sure Aunt Minnie will give a musicale or a Venetian breakfast or some such for you. You will probably just be at Bronston House to sleep."

"I wish I could stay with you."

Michael laughed, still trying to cheer her up. "You would not like that at all, Vi, I assure you! My lodgings are not at all up to the standards of *A Lady's Rules*. You would be most appalled."

She giggled, a good sign. "I am sure it is *horrid*. Tell me about it, Michael."

For the rest of their drive, Michael regaled her with exaggerated tales of the decrepitude of his rooms. His descriptions of piles of dirty laundry and thick dust on the bookshelves made her laugh. By the time they drew to a halt outside Bronston House, her eyes were clearer and her cheeks pink.

Her laughter faded as she stared up at its forbidding gray stone façade, and she reached up to touch her locket. "Will you stay for tea, Michael?" she asked quietly.

"Of course I will, Vi," he answered. He handed the reins to a footman, and jumped down to come around and help her to the ground. "And I will take you to supper at Aunt Minnie's tonight, too, if you want."

"Oh, yes!" she agreed enthusiastically. "I would like that very much."

Michael offered her his arm, and together they climbed the front steps to the door of Bronston House—or, as Michael chose to think of it, the portal of doom.

The Seminary was so quiet with all the girls gone, Rosalind thought. A bit *too* quiet, perhaps. For the first day or two of a holiday she was never quite sure what to do with herself.

She sat alone in her private sitting room after supper, with a tea tray on the table beside her and an open workbasket at her feet. Miss James, the only teacher still at the school, had taken supper with Rosalind, but then retired to pack for her own holiday.

So Rosalind was alone, with only the crackle of the flames in the grate to break the silence. Usually, in the evenings, she would listen to the girls play the harp or the pianoforte, or examine their watercolors and needlework. She tried to make the Seminary a home atmosphere for them, a place where they could be comfortable and happy.

Why could the home atmosphere not be here for *her* as well, even when they were gone? Why was it so very *silent*?

Nonsense, she told herself. She was just being maudlin. This happened every time a holiday commenced. Of course this was her home, the finest home she had ever known. And there were many things she could be doing. Things such as working on a new edition of *A Lady's Rules,* which her publisher had requested.

Thinking of *A Lady's Rules* made her remember that scene in her office, where she had presented a copy to Lord Morley. The expression on his face had been mocking, arch—after a flash of what, on another person, might have been hurt. It had been gone in an instant, yet Rosalind still felt the vague stirrings of regret when she remembered it.

Did she herself not have a rule against making guests feel uncomfortable in her home? Yet she had practically accused the man of uncouth rudeness, which was *not* the done thing.

"Even if it *is* true," she whispered, staring into the flames.

The first time she met Lord Morley she *had* been appalled by his manners. But she had to admit, today he had behaved better. Much better. There had been no lolling in the chairs, no suggestive poetry, no winking at housemaids. This afternoon, aside from lifting his sister off of her feet when he greeted her, he had been a picture of the *Rules*. Almost. He could never be completely.

And he had been truly kind when she felt ill. She had repaid his kindness by thrusting the book at him and practically accusing him of being a baboon.

"What has become of you, Rosalind?" she asked herself, not caring that it was ridiculous to be talking to an empty room in such a manner. "You are only thirty years of age, but you act worse than your grandmother ever did."

She sighed when she recalled their cheerless childhood visits to Grandmother Allen, their mother's mother who had been the sister of an earl and never let anyone forget it. Grandmother Allen insisted children sit perfectly straight and still and silent. How she and her brother had hated those calls!

Was she now *becoming* their Grandmother Allen?

Rosalind shuddered, and stood up to walk over to the fireplace. Of course she was not becoming her grandmother. She merely placed a great importance on manners, on proper deportment, and there was nothing wrong with that.

She braced her hand on the carved wooden mantel, and studied the miniature portrait displayed there on its silver stand. Her late husband, Mr. Charles Chase, stared back at her with his frank blue gaze. "There is nothing wrong with that, is there, Charles?"

She fancied that his smile widened. Charles, a very proper village attorney, had also believed in the importance of propriety, despite his occasional whiskey or card game. It was what had brought them together, had sustained them through their too-short three years of marriage before Charles succumbed to a fever.

A perfectly proper three years. They had been friends, even if theirs had not been a romance for the ages.

Rosalind's gaze shifted from the portrait to the book she had laid on the mantel before supper.

Lord Morley's poetry.

Rosalind reached for it, wrapped her fingers around the rich brown leather cover. She should have left it downstairs in the library, but some compulsion had made her bring it up here before she ate. For some light, before-bed reading, perhaps?

She opened the volume to a random page, and read, "Her lips, two roses touched with morning dew . . ."

Rosalind snapped the book shut. The fire felt so warm, *too* warm. She turned away, still holding the book, and went to the window.

She had not yet drawn the draperies, even though it was full dark now. The moon was almost full, and cast a greenish silver glow over the garden. The grounds looked lovely, just as they ought to.

Rosalind rested her forehead against the cool glass of the window, letting the blessed familiarity of the scene into her heart. This was what she wanted, what she had always wanted. The familiar, the known, the proper.

Why, then, did her fingers close so tightly about the book she held? So tightly that its corner bit into her palm?

She closed her eyes for a moment. When she opened them, the scene in the garden was the same—except for a new shadow falling from behind one of the trees. It flickered and moved, not a part of the tree's own solid shadow at all.

But when Rosalind blinked and peered closer, it was gone.

"Now you are seeing ghosts, in addition to everything else," she muttered. She stepped back and pulled the draperies firmly closed.

No sooner had she settled the yellow taffeta draperies than the door opened, and Molly, the housemaid, came in. Rosalind was deeply grateful for her cheerful smile, her bob of a curtsy—it made the evening seem *right,* somehow, after poetry and ghosts.

"Have you finished with the tea things, ma'am?" Molly asked.

"Oh, yes, thank you, Molly. I am done with them."
Rosalind watched the maid as she gathered up the
tray. "Molly?"

"Yes, ma'am."

"None of the gardeners are still here, are they?"

Molly seemed surprised by the question, as well she
might. Why would anyone be asking about gardeners
at nine o'clock at night? "No, ma'am. It's just you and
me and Miss James now."

"Oh, yes, of course."

Molly lifted up the tea tray. Before she turned back
to the door, she said, "I'll come right back, ma'am,
and help you with your gown, if you're ready to
retire."

"Yes, thank you, Molly." Rosalind rubbed her hand
over her eyes. She *was* ready to retire—obviously, she
was in need of some sleep. Exhaustion was making
her fanciful.

She had been reading one of Mrs. More's edifying
epistles before she went to sleep. But perhaps tonight
she might take a peek at some more of that poetry . . .

Chapter Five

"Parents and other elders should always be respected."
—*A Lady's Rules for Proper Behavior*, Chapter Seven

"So, here you are at last. I thought that with the harum-skarum way *you* drive, Michael, that you would have been here hours ago."

The Earl of Athley's voice, stentorian as a brass gong, rang through the cavernous drawing room as Michael and Violet stepped inside the door. Michael squinted through the gloom of the room, until he saw his father seated by the fire.

As usual the drawing room, indeed the whole house, was dark and stuffy, the air thick with smoke and the overpowering sweetness of the rose and orchid flower arrangements. Heavy green velvet draperies, hung with swags of gold fringe, covered all the windows. More green velvet upholstered the dark, old-fashioned furniture, and gloomy landscapes hung on the paneled walls.

It was overpowering, suffocating. Michael felt his chest tighten painfully, his throat close as if gasping for a breath of clear, true air.

He felt this way every time he entered the house. And that was why he stayed far, far away, unless his duty to his sister pulled him back. At least he could leave—she could not.

He reached up to loosen his cravat slightly, as Violet's hand slipped from his arm and she crossed the room to their father's side. Her lilac-colored carriage gown and white bonnet were like a flash of springtime dropped into the gloom.

She leaned down to peck a dutiful kiss onto the earl's wrinkled cheek. "It was my fault we are late, Father. I stayed too long at the school, saying good-bye to everyone."

The earl scowled. "Who at that pitiful Seminary could have been worth your taking all that time? Some parson's daughter or merchant's niece?" He banged his stout walking stick on the floor, the hollow thud of it echoing up to the rafters. "I was a fool to ever send you to that school, Violet. I should not have listened to your aunt's blandishments. Associating with people of all sorts has obviously made you forget your position. You should be here, learning to prepare for marriage. What else are girls good for?"

Violet turned panicked eyes onto Michael.

Michael came toward her, breathing a bit easier now that he had somewhat adjusted to the dimness. He understood Violet's panic—the Seminary, as fusty as it was, was her refuge from this place. But he was not as worried as she. Their father often ranted about the school, about Violet's "forgetting her position" there, getting too educated and not being able to find a suit-able husband because of it. Yet the truth was, the earl would rather not have the trouble of his daughter being underfoot. So her school was safe—for now.

"Father, you know that the Seminary has only stu-dents from the finest families enrolled there," Michael said, gently taking Violet's arm and leading her to a chair away from the overpowering heat of the fire. "Violet has only the most suitable friends, who will be of great help to her when she makes her debut next Season."

Michael had almost said "use" rather than "help," since that was all the earl truly cared about in peo-ple—how he could use them to his advantage. How they were placed on the social scale. "I understand,

Father, that the Duke and Duchess of Wayland are sending their own daughter there in few years."

"Wayland, eh?" The earl's dark eyes narrowed shrewdly as he absorbed this. The Waylands were assuredly at the pinnacle of Society. "Well, that at least is something. Though I do not know what they are thinking to send their daughter there so early. There is no telling what odd notions the gel might absorb there. But then, the Waylands are odd people. The duchess is an *artist*." His lips curled with disdain on the word *artist*—it might as well have been *courtesan*.

As their father went on, dissecting the peccadilloes of the Waylands and their "disgraceful" set, Michael sat down in the chair next to Violet's. He leaned back, trying to get comfortable in the heavily carved piece of furniture, stretching his legs out before him. Violet was rubbing her fingertip over her silver locket, staring at the floor. She was the very picture of a dutiful daughter, but Michael recognized the misty look in her eyes as one of faraway thought. She was lost in some daydream, so Michael tried to follow her example and think of something else.

Their father's conversation seldom required more of a response than a nod, or an "Oh, yes?" or a "You are quite right, sir." So distraction was fairly easy. His gaze moved over the half-hidden footman standing in a shadowed corner to await the earl's command, to the large stone coat of arms over the fireplace. It had the Bronston insignia of a hand holding a sword and a lion, with the motto *Semper Officiosus.*

Duty Always. Perhaps, Michael thought, it should have been *Dullness Always.* He almost wished he could trade places with that footman.

His musings were interrupted when he heard his name.

"Michael," the earl barked, "is that a *pink* cravat you are wearing?"

Michael grinned. "Indeed. Though the correct name is 'maiden's blush.' Quite evocative, wouldn't you say? It is all the crack."

Violet made a suspicious choking sound, and bent her head down until her expression was entirely concealed by the brim of her bonnet.

The earl turned a deep red color, one that would never earn a moniker like "maiden's blush." "Miser's apoplexy," perhaps.

"Insolent!" the earl shouted, and banged the stick against the floor again. "I have put up with your deplorable behavior thus far, your 'poetry,' your 'club,' the tittle-tattle I hear from every quarter. Even your ridiculous notions about fashion! But I will not stand your disgraceful behavior any longer. You are a viscount, and one day you will be the earl . . ." He broke off, gasping for air. The footman hurried forward to pour out a glass of some clear liquid, which the earl gulped down.

"Father!" Violet cried, and started to rise from her chair.

"Sit back down, gel!" her father choked. "I am not finished with what I have to say."

"But you are ill," Violet dared to say.

"A mere shortness of breath. I am not dying, which is a very good thing, considering the disgraceful state of the next generation. The family will be ruined before I am cold in the ground."

Violet's face crumpled with hurt at those words. She sank back into her chair.

Michael's hands tightened onto the arms of his own chair until his knuckles whitened. His father had always been cold, hateful, haughty to those not of his own station—and even to his own children. Ever since his wife died bringing Violet into the world, he had revealed no hint of human feeling. But age had brought a new venom to him, a deep anger.

Michael had never met a man more in need of a good thrashing. But his father was indeed an old man—it would not be at all honorable for Michael, with all the strength of his twenty-eight years, to beat him.

Really, he thought, all he would have to do now was steal the earl's walking stick. Even *that* could not be done, but one day Michael would tell him every last truth he had coming to him. Every last hateful thought that Michael harbored in his own heart.

Not now, though, with his sweet Violet looking on. Michael would never do anything that could possibly hurt his tenderhearted sister.

Before the earl could launch into another diatribe, Michael stood up and said, "I am sorry to cut short this cozy family moment, but I fear I have errands I must perform. I told Violet I would take her to Aunt Minnie's house for supper, so you need not share your dried-out lamb cutlets and overcooked peas with us. Good day, sir."

"I will just see you out, Michael," Violet said hurriedly. Together they left the room as quickly as dignity would allow, their father's sputterings chasing them out the door.

"How absolutely horrid," said Violet, shuddering, once they stood safely on the front steps. "He becomes worse every time I see him!"

Michael kissed her cheek, and she curled her hands into the folds of his coat, holding onto him in defiance of her precious rules.

"It will be all right, Vi," he said reassuringly. "Do not go back to the drawing room. Go up to your chamber, and send your maid for some tea. Father will settle down now that my infuriating presence has been removed. I will be back in only a couple of hours, and we will have a lovely supper with Aunt Minnie and her friends. Does that sound nice?"

"Very nice." Violet nodded, and stepped back to give him a brave little smile.

"Now go inside. It is becoming chilly out here." Michael tapped Violet on the tip of her nose, and climbed up into his phaeton.

At the corner of the street, he glanced back to be sure she had gone inside. She had not. She still stood there on the steps, her arms wrapped around herself.

She gave him a wave, and another smile—and Michael's heart ached. He wanted so very much to go back to her, to sweep her up and carry her away from that gloomy house.

Carry her all the way back to the serenity of Mrs. Chase's drawing room. Mrs. Chase would be able to comfort Violet. And what was even odder, he wished *he* could be there, as well. That he could sit in that small office again, and tell Mrs. Chase all the things that ached in his soul. Not the stern, stiff schoolmistress Mrs. Chase, but the one he had glimpsed so briefly. The one with rich depths to her sky-eyes, and soft hands and sunset hair. That Mrs. Chase had hints of gentleness and understanding in her.

Instead, all he could do was keep driving into the gathering London night.

The townhouse of Lady Minerva Fielding, better known as Aunt Minnie, was as different from Bronston House as day was from midnight. She was their father's sister, but she had lived a very different life from his, as evidenced in the spacious, pastel airiness of her rooms, the fine paintings on her walls, the constant merry sparkle in her green eyes.

She was one of the last people Michael would ever have expected to follow *A Lady's Rules,* but there the volume was, in a place of honor on the round table in the middle of her foyer.

As Violet hurried off to greet some of Aunt Minnie's other guests, Michael picked up the book, riffling through its gilt-edged pages. Their aunt had marked certain "rules" with ticks of dark green ink.

" 'A gentleman must never seat himself on the settee beside his hostess . . . unless invited,' " he muttered.

"Michael!" Aunt Minnie cried. He looked up to find her sailing out of the drawing room doors toward him, the tall feathers in her rose pink turban waving jauntily. She went up on tiptoe to kiss his cheek. "My most handsome nephew."

Michael laughed, and kissed her in return. "I am your only nephew."

She waved this away with an airy gesture of her gloved hand. "If I had a hundred nephews, you would still be the most handsome. You are becoming quite the heartbreaker, so I hear."

"Exaggerations, I assure you, aunt."

"Hmm," she murmured, clearly unconvinced. "Exaggerations, perhaps. But obviously it runs in the family, as Violet is also becoming a very pretty figure. It is obvious that Mrs. Chase's Seminary agrees with her. She is blooming."

Michael glanced over to where Violet was chatting with an elderly colonel and his wife. She was smiling, and as bright and pretty as her yellow muslin gown. It was reassuring that she had emerged unscathed from their meeting with their father—at least for now. "It was thanks to your persuasions that our father agreed to send her there."

Aunt Minnie gave an inelegant snort. "Oh, my brother is terrible, and has been ever since we were children! But Violet seems to be weathering the storm, as do you, my dear."

"Violet will *always* be fine, because she has inherited your beauty and good heart. As well as your literary taste, I believe?" He held up the copy of *A Lady's Rules.*

She laughed, and snatched the volume out of his hand. "It is all anyone is reading of late! I haven't seen a craze to equal it in years, not since I was a girl and everyone had to wear heart-shaped patches. To be au courant now one must be *polite.* Such a bore, not at all like the great fun we had in my youth. Wigs a foot tall, high heels, card games that lasted a week, not to mention those patches. But the *Rules* are really quite amusing to peruse. I can loan you my copy."

"No need, Aunt Minnie. I was recently given a copy of my very own." Michael remembered the expression on Mrs. Chase's face as she held the book out to him. *"You in particular are most in need of it, Lord Morley."*

Aunt Minnie gave him an arch glance. "Oh, yes? And may I venture a guess that it was a gift from a lady?"

Michael gave her a *look* of his own. "You may venture as many guesses as you like, Aunt Minnie. A gentleman never tells. Is that one of the rules?"

She laughed again. "If it is not, it should be! But come with me, young rascal. We have been standing here for too long, and there are guests I would like you to meet."

As she took his arm to lead him into the fray of her company, Michael took another glance at the book before tossing it back onto the table. *A Lady's Rules*—they were everywhere.

Chapter Six

"A lady should always try to avoid discussing such matters as finances and politics."
—*A Lady's Rules for Proper Behavior,* Chapter Two

"*T*he morning post has come, ma'am," Molly announced, putting a small silver tray down on Rosalind's desk.

Rosalind glanced up from her writing, automatically sliding a blank sheet of vellum over her notebook. It was not that she didn't trust Molly—it was simply instinct. She was working on the new edition of *A Lady's Rules,* which her publisher had been trying for weeks to get her to begin. She had to preserve her anonymity as A Lady.

"Thank you, Molly," she said, and reached for the sheaf of letters.

"Would you like your luncheon in here, ma'am, or in the dining room?" the maid asked.

Rosalind did not need very long to make *that* decision. It was much too gloomy to eat all alone in the spacious dining room. During the term, it was full of people, students practicing their table manners under the watchful gaze of the teachers, their talk and laughter ringing out. During the holiday, it was silent.

"In here, please, Molly. I am going to try to work through the afternoon."

"Very good, ma'am." Molly bobbed a curtsy and left the office, closing the door behind her.

Rosalind sorted through the post. There were a couple of missives from her teachers, on their holidays in Bath and Lyme Regis. A few notes from parents inquiring about future places at the school for their daughters. A scribbled, blotted note from Uncle Silas at his country home.

And one frighteningly official-looking letter from the bank in London. The one Allen had borrowed money from.

Rosalind stared down at the green blob of wax on the heavy white vellum. As she stared, the wax shifted, twisted, until it looked like a yawning, gaping, *biting* tiger's jaw. Poised to swallow her, and her comfortable world, whole.

She slid a letter opener under the wax wafer, popping it open, and unfolded the sheet.

It was short, polite, and to the point. Mr. Richards, one of the managers of the bank, would very much appreciate an appointment with her and Mr. Silas Lucas, to discuss recent loans made to Mr. Allen Lucas. Sincerely hers, etc. . . .

Rosalind dropped the letter to her desk. The skin around her eyes tightened painfully at the thought of having to meet with some *bank manager*. It sounded, well, less than respectable. Not something a lady should have to face. It reeked of financial ruin. She took off her wire-framed spectacles and rubbed at the bridge of her nose.

Blast Allen anyway. He had no right to put her through this. This was the fault of Lord Morley, and others of his reprehensible ilk. If not for their influence, Allen would be quietly studying, not running up debts.

What was she going to do about this mess?

The Thoth Club was crowded on this Wednesday night, thronged with gentlemen freed at this late hour from their duties of escorting wives, sisters, and sweethearts to the dreaded Almack's. Brandy was liberal, the billiards room full, the card tables surrounded by players and observers.

Michael sat in one of the comfortable wingback
chairs by the fireplace, a glass of port cradled in his
hands, watching the hum of activity. He himself had
just passed an evening in respectable society, escorting
Violet and Aunt Minnie to a small musicale. Not,
thankfully, to Almack's—Vi was still too young for its
hallowed portals—but still heavy with propriety. Now
Violet was left with Aunt Minnie and her cronies in
Minnie's drawing room, and Michael was here, in this
masculine sanctuary.

Sanctuary? Strangely, it felt like a mere extension
of the outside world.

Michael sipped at his port, and tried to decipher
why this place, which had always been a place of en-
joyment and escape for him ever since he helped to
found it, should feel so cold tonight. He had always
enjoyed the Thoth Club. It was full of members with
an artistic or literary bent, not like politically minded
Whites and Brooks, or sporting-mad Boodle's. There
was always discussion of Byron's latest volume or
Turner's newest canvas to go along with the cards and
drink. Even the food was not half bad.

Tonight, though, he felt oddly—restless. He did not
want to play cards, or talk about poetry, or do any of
the things that usually sufficed to while away a pleasant evening. Ordinarily it was all amusing enough,
even if not profoundly satisfying. Tonight, though, it
was just not enough. He briefly considered visiting the
home of a most obliging golden-haired courtesan, but
not even that appealed to him.

He should leave, go back to his lodgings and write.
In his own world of words and fantasies, time could
often fly past on silvery wings. That was sometimes
the only thing that could satisfy him, the ephemeral
zone of art. It was far, far beyond the shallow pas-
times of gaming, horse races, balls—even blond cour-
tesans. Tonight, though, he felt that even poetry
could not fill the hollowness at the very center of
his being.

So he just sat there, sipping at the glass of port, watching the activity of the club swirl past him.

The front doors opened, letting in a burst of cool evening air and a flurry of new arrivals. They were laughing brightly, talking too loudly—obviously, they had begun their carousing long before coming to the club.

Among them was Allen Lucas.

"Morley!" Lucas cried upon seeing Michael. He handed his cloak and hat to the footman, and staggered across the room to collapse in the chair next to Michael's. He paid no attention to Michael's obvious solitude, gesturing for a port of his own.

"How are you this evening, Lucas?" Michael asked, and put his half-empty glass down on the nearest table. Apparently, alcohol was going to be of no use to him this evening.

"Very well indeed. Haven't seen you since that day at m'sister's school." Lucas tossed off his first drink, and poured out another from the decanter. He loosened his elaborately fashioned cravat. "I didn't know your sister attended the Seminary."

"Oh, yes. Lady Violet enjoys it there very much."

Lucas snorted. "I daresay she does. All the girls just *worship* Rosie."

"Hm," Michael murmured noncommittally. He really did not want to think about Mrs. Chase this night. Lately, every time he closed his eyes he saw her disapproving face, her blue eyes watching him with disappointment. He did not know why that should be; he had only met the woman twice in his life. And neither encounter had been what could be called auspicious. But there it was—he *had* been thinking of her, and he wanted to escape it.

And now here was the woman's very own brother, sitting down right across from him. *I need a distraction,* he thought.

Fortunately, he was saved from hearing any more about "Rosie" by the arrival of two of Lucas's cronies, Lord Carteret and Mr. Gilmore.

"Good evening, Morley!" Gilmore said, helping himself to the port. "Damn shame you didn't come out with us earlier."

"Oh, yes? Where did you go?" Michael replied, not deeply interested in the answer. But as long as the silly puppies were here, they might as well keep him entertained.

"We were at Lady Lovelace's rout," Carteret said, with a small hiccup. "And she threw us out!"

Now, that *was* a bit interesting, Michael thought. Lady Lovelace was not a woman generally known for being a high stickler, so this trio must have done something rather naughty indeed. "She threw you out?"

"Tossed us right out on our ears," Lucas said, laughing into his port.

"Why?" Michael asked. "What did you do?"

Carteret leaned his elbow lazily on the edge of the mantel. "She said we were breaking the rules."

The rules! Of course. Michael gave a bitter little laugh. Only something as ridiculous as "the rules" could get three such harmless pups expelled from the Lovelace rout. They were spreading like a virulent weed over Society, choking out any trace of individuality, any spark that could possibly enliven dull *ton* events.

"She said that the rules forbid a gentleman from being intoxicated in front of a lady," Lucas said indignantly. "We were hardly *foxed*! How could one be, on that weak stuff Lady Lovelace serves?"

"And when I tried to tell a simple joke to Lady Lovelace's daughter, the silly gel squealed like an affronted mouse, and ran off to tell her mama," added Gilmore. "It was just the one about the opera dancer and the clock at St. Sebastian's . . ."

"Lady Lovelace pulled out a copy of *A Lady's Rules* and spouted off something about tasteless anecdotes," said Lucas.

"Tasteless!" Gilmore cried. "That was my very best joke. It always gets a laugh."

"Hm." Michael studied the flames leaping in the grate, as the three young men went on muttering about their "shabby" treatment at the hands of Lady Lovelace.

It was true that their behavior had not been all that it should have been, Michael admitted. Drinking too much and telling questionable stories to young ladies was *not* the done thing. But they were harmless young men, and had meant nothing by it. Their behavior had surely warranted their being taken outside by Lord Lovelace into the fresh air to sober up, but *not* being tossed publicly out of the soiree.

"It is those blasted rules," Gilmore said, echoing Michael's own thoughts. "Ever since Lady Jersey and the other patronesses started touting them all over the place, everyone is wild to follow them to the exact letter."

"It's dashed hard," Lucas complained. "I can never remember all of them at once, so I'm always bound to break at least one."

"But one *has* to follow them," said Carteret gloomily. "If one wants to be accepted. As dull as all those routs and balls are, I want to be able to attend them. That is where all the pretty girls are, and my father would cut off my allowance if I didn't do my duty there."

"We just have to try harder to remember the rules," said Lucas.

Here was the distraction he sought, Michael realized.

They all fell into a maudlin silence, broken only when Michael said quietly, "Not necessarily, gentlemen."

The three of them turned in concert to stare at him, three pairs of eyes wide.

"What do you mean, Morley?" asked Lucas.

"Well, you say that a person cannot be accepted in Society unless he follows all these rules," Michael said, and tapped thoughtfully at his chin with his steepled fingers. "Yet it seems to me that the people who have commanded the most attention, indeed the adulation, of the *ton* have been anything but rule followers."

The trio brightened, leaning toward Michael avidly to hear what he might say next. "You mean like you, Morley?" Lucas asked.

Michael laughed. "I was thinking more of Byron, or perhaps Beau Brummell, who made his own rules and everyone followed *them*. These men, and others like them, would never have slavishly followed any rules in some book. Why, this lady will not even put her name on her own book! How much importance can her rules truly have, if she won't even own up to them?"

Gilmore appeared most confused. "You mean we should write our own book of rules and get people to follow them?"

"I don't think I could write a book. Not bright enough, y'know," Carteret added doubtfully.

Michael almost groaned in exasperation. No wonder he was restless, if these bacon-brains were the only people he had to converse with! But somehow he felt he had to persuade them, to save at least three helpless souls from more mindless rule-following. "No, I do not mean write your own rules. I mean forget about rules entirely. If we follow common courtesy, and our own instincts, we will be fine. If you go a step beyond, and follow a different path, you will be admired."

"Like you, Morley," Lucas insisted again. "The ladies love it that you never do what is expected."

"They *did* love it," Gilmore said, his voice slurred from the great quantity of port he had consumed. "But I haven't seen you out much of late, Morley, and you weren't at the Lovelace rout tonight."

"That is because he did not *choose* to waste his time at such a dull place as Lady Lovelace's rout!" Lucas cried. "She would have given her right arm to have him there, as would every Society hostess. Morley is right. Some people are above the rules."

Michael had rarely had champions in his life, and never one as unlikely as Allen Lucas. But it was rather touching all the same.

"The lady who wrote the book says *no one* is above the rules," Gilmore insisted.

"No one is above courtesy, perhaps," said Michael. "But no one should slavishly follow someone else's commands."

"I would wager that not even *you* can flout the rules and still be accepted, Morley," argued Gilmore. "They are too popular."

Lucas leaped to his feet to face Gilmore, his face flushed a deep red. "And I would wager that Morley will *always* be accepted, no matter how many rules he breaks! I wager fifty pounds."

"Done!" Gilmore answered.

Carteret glanced between them, laconically gleeful at the quarrel.

Michael studied the three of them in silence, tapping his fingertips on the arms of his chair. The wager was completely ridiculous, of course; Michael had outgrown betting on such silly matters years ago. But the rules had irked him, probably more than they should have. He hated seeing everyone, especially his sweet sister, behaving like such wooden soldiers, marching in the cause of rigid etiquette. It reminded him too much of his father.

Plus, this would give him a chance to get—and keep—his thoughts off of Mrs. Chase.

"Very well, gentlemen," he said. "I will take that wager."

Chapter Seven

"Correspondence is a private matter, and one
must never read another person's letters without
being invited."
—*A Lady's Rules for Proper Behavior*, Chapter Six

"*T*here is a caller, ma'am."

Rosalind glanced up from her embroidery to
see Molly in the doorway of the sitting room. "A
caller?" she said, puzzled. It was early on a quiet
morning, and Rosalind had been enjoying the time
to make some progress on her needlework while she
pondered Allen and some new expenses at the school.
She had not heard from her brother for several days,
and it was beginning to worry her. Also, the roof had
begun to leak in the east wing, and the funds would
have to be found to repair it.

She always thought more clearly with a piece of
embroidery in her hands. But today, no solutions were
occurring to her. She was almost grateful to be interrupted, even if it was not the usual time for callers.

"Who is it, Molly?" she asked, and tucked her embroidery away into her workbasket.

Molly came to her and held out the silver tray,
where one stark white card reposed. "He says his
name is Mr. Richards. From the bank."

Rosalind's hand froze as she reached for the card.
Mr. Richards. The one who had been writing her letters about Allen's stupid loan. Now he was here, in

person. He must be quite serious if he took all the trouble to come out here to the school.

She grasped the card, and folded it into her hand until it bit into her palm. "Tell him I will be down momentarily, Molly."

Molly bobbed a curtsy, and left the room with her empty tray.

Safely alone now, Rosalind took a deep breath of air. She hated dealing with finances, except for paying bills with the local tradesmen at the end of the month. Those were simple, straightforward, necessary transactions. Her experiences with Allen's creditors in the past had proved to be anything *but* simple.

And this was the first time she had had to face a banker from London.

Rosalind straightened her muslin cap and smoothed the skirt of her gray morning gown. He would not go away if she just kept hiding in here. She had to meet him, work out some sort of payment plan for Allen's loans.

Oh, she was just going to *strangle* her brother when next she saw him!

She squared her shoulders and marched down the stairs to the drawing room.

Rosalind had never given much thought to what bankers should look like, but if she *had,* it would be much like this man. He was very tall, very thin, and very pale—pale skin, pale blond hair. He wore a plain dark blue coat, and a stiff white cravat tucked into the front of a black waistcoat. He stood across the room, examining a collection of small porcelain figurines and boxes arrayed on a tabletop.

"Mr. Richards?" she said, drawing herself up to her full, tall height and walking toward him, her hand outstretched. "I am Mrs. Rosalind Chase."

Mr. Richards straightened from his examination of the bibelots, a monocle falling from his eye. "Mrs. Chase," he said, and bowed briefly over her hand. "I was really hoping to speak with both you and Mr. Silas Lucas."

"My uncle is quite elderly now, and not in the best of health. He seldom leaves his home in the country. But I assure you that, as co-guardian of my brother, I have the authority to speak to you myself. Please, won't you be seated?" She gestured toward a pair of chairs.

"Of course, Mrs. Chase," Mr. Richards said, clearly still reluctant. He sat down, and placed a large black leather portfolio across his lap. From it he withdrew a stack of papers. At the bottom of the top sheet Rosalind saw, with a sinking of her heart, the bold slash of Allen's signature.

"These are the documents pertaining to Mr. Lucas's loan," Mr. Richards began. "As you see here, Mrs. Chase . . ."

He went on in this vein for some time, spouting different legal terms and quoting figures.

A suspicious throbbing began above her left eye, until she had to say, "Please, Mr. Richards. Could you please just tell me what I must do to repay this loan?"

Two hours later, when she collapsed onto the settee in her office, Rosalind was very sorry she had asked that question. She had indeed worked out a repayment plan with Mr. Richards and his bank, but it was not going to be quick or simple. The school was prosperous, yes, but it could not long support such debts. The building and grounds of the Seminary also required upkeep, not to mention the wages of the teachers and servants.

Her head ached in earnest now, as it had so often of late. She pressed the heels of her hands against her temples.

"Oh, Allen, Allen!" she groaned. "What were you thinking of? Where did I go wrong?"

But she knew in her heart that it was not her fault. She had tried hard to teach him the values of education and thrift. He had fallen in with a bad example of behavior in London.

He had fallen in with Lord Morley and his crowd.

At the thought of that name, her head pounded harder. She could *not* think of him now! She had to conserve her energy for what truly mattered—finding a solution to her financial dilemma.

She pushed herself up off the settee and went over to the desk to pull out her ledger books. One detailed the school's finances, the other the profits from *A Lady's Rules*.

"I will just have to write more books," she murmured, and reached for her pen and ink. "A Lady's Rules for Fashion? A Lady's Rules for Garden Design?"

As she sharpened the tip of the pen, her gaze fell on the new pile of letters on the edge of the desk. The morning post. Molly must have left it there when Rosalind was in the drawing room with Mr. Richards.

She did not really want to face correspondence on top of everything else, but the missive on top appeared to be a letter from her school friend, Georgina Beaumont, now the Duchess of Wayland and cutting a dash in London. Georgie would surely have gossip to cheer her! Reading of her adventures always lifted Rosalind's spirits.

Rosalind pulled the post toward her, anticipating a respite from her woes. But the letter just beneath Georgina's was a missive from her publisher.

"Oh, thank heaven!" she whispered, breaking the wax with her letter opener. "There is sure to be a bank draught."

There *was* a draught—yet it was not nearly large enough. It was only half what her previous payments had been. Appalled, she put aside the bank draught and read her publisher's letter.

"We apologize for the unexpectedly small sum," it read. "Unfortunately, sales of *A Lady's Rules* have inexplicably dropped. We would be very happy to look at any other manuscripts you may have to offer. Yours, etc. . . ."

"What!" Rosalind screamed out, and dropped the paper as if it burned. "Sales have dropped? What can this mean? *Everyone* wants to read *A Lady's Rules*."

Did they not? They had become so very popular.

This was the worst possible time for something of this nature to happen. She was counting on that money—she *needed* it. She had known that the popularity of *A Lady's Rules* would one day wane, but not so very soon. Not *now*.

Lights exploded in her brain, pounding at the inside of her skull. Rosalind pushed the letter away, not caring when it fell to the floor. She felt so—trapped. Unable to break out of this dilemma. It was even worse than it had been when her husband died, and she discovered that his estate was far smaller than she had thought.

She needed some air.

Tucking Georgina's letter into the pocket of her morning gown, Rosalind stumbled out of the office, across the empty foyer. She pulled open the front door and walked blindly out into the garden.

At first the pale sunlight hurt her eyes, made her headache worse. But the breeze was cool and clear, the garden an early spring pale green. Slowly, as she filled her lungs with its country freshness, she felt calmer. More in charge of herself.

She sat down on a marble bench beneath a spreading oak tree, and pulled Georgina's letter from her pocket.

Her hope for distraction was not in vain. Georgina's usual effervescence, which had carried them through some difficult school days, came across in her words. Rosalind soon found herself smiling at Georgina's stories of her young daughter and baby son, her sister-in-law's come-out, gossip about her friends, including their fellow school friend Elizabeth Hollingsworth, who was traveling in Italy with her husband and twin daughters. Rosalind even laughed aloud at a particularly spicy tale of a certain Lord Bunberry and Mrs. Brown-Perkins, even though she knew she shouldn't.

Her laughter faded at Georgina's final paragraph, though.

"And, in closing, my dear Rosie, something most odd is happening. You know of *A Lady's Rules for Proper Behavior,* that amusing little book everyone has been so wild to follow of late? Even *I* have improved my etiquette! Well, Lord Morley and some of his cronies have been behaving just so badly of late. It is as if they are trying to break every rule. Everyone is absolutely agog to see what they will do next. I will write more of this later, for I think it will grow even more interesting."

Morley! Rosalind wanted to scream that name to the wind. It was always Morley, popping up whenever she was most vulnerable. Ruining all her plans, her good work. He was becoming the bane of her life, setting himself up against every civilized tenet that Rosalind stood for.

She tightened her grip on the letter, crumpling it into her fist. There was just one thing to be done. She had to go to London.

Chapter Eight

"A crowded ball is not the proper sphere for private conversation."
A Lady's Rules for Proper Behavior,   Chapter Three

*T*he Portman ball was quite the crush. People thronged along the silk-papered walls, lined the staircase to the ballroom, jostled across the corridors in order to greet Lord and Lady Portman and proceed into the soiree. The crème de la crème of Society was arrayed in all its glittering, silken splendor.

And they all turned to stare when the butler announced, "Viscount Morley."

There was a tiny pause, a sort of collective murmur before talk resumed in one great rush. Lady Portman and several of her friends rushed forward to greet him.

It was slightly disconcerting. Michael was used to a certain amount of attention, as any unmarried heir to an earldom would be, but not *this* much attention. It was gratifying, too. At least he knew his wager was going well. People still associated with him, indeed fawned on him, even though he tried to break all of *A Lady's Rules* whenever possible.

Well, not *all* of them. There were still two or three he had not gotten around to. But it was early days yet. Surely, given time, everyone would see how absurd such rules were. Even Violet, who had been watching him with narrowed, disapproving eyes of late. Ever since his rule-breaking had begun in earnest.

His sister, his sweet, pliant sister, was clinging tenaciously to every strict tenet that she had learned at that blasted school. Every conversation, it was Mrs. Chase this, and Mrs. Chase that, Mrs. Chase says this, Mrs. Chase does that.

Always Mrs. Chase. The rule-following Mrs. Chase.

He frowned as he thought of her again. The memory of Mrs. Chase came into his mind at the most inopportune moments, ever since that strangely intimate scene in her office. He would be at the theater, and an actress's red hair would remind him of the ringlet that had escaped from Mrs. Chase's cap. He would be riding in the park, and a whiff of some springtime scent would make him think of her perfume, so green and fresh when he leaned close to her. He was even at a prizefight, and—well, he was not sure *what* had reminded him of her at that violent scene, but he had thought of her nonetheless.

It was absurd. Ridiculous. Mrs. Chase was a stern, cap-wearing schoolmistress, who looked at him with the highest disapproval. She had even given him a copy of *A Lady's Rules*! She was not at all the usual sort of woman he was drawn to—blond, giggling, vivacious, petite. Mrs. Chase was a tall, redheaded Valkyrie.

Yet there it was. He could not cease thinking about her—even now, at a grand ball, surrounded by females. Her ice blue eyes lingered in his mind. It was almost as if she watched him across the miles, disapproving of him.

He shook off the thought of Mrs. Chase, and turned to Lady Portman. "Good evening, Lady Portman," he said, bowing low over her gloved hand. He lingered over it just an instant more than was proper, mindful that the rules required the merest airy salute. "You have quite outdone yourself this evening. Your ball is the event of the Season."

Lady Portman gave a gay little trill of laughter, and tapped him on the arm with her folded lace fan. "You flatterer! I am sure it cannot be *the* event of the Season, but it has surely moved closer because you are here, Lord Morley. Perhaps you could read us one of your new poems after supper?"

"Oh, yes!" Lady Portman's friend Mrs. Eastman cried. She laid a beseeching hand on his other arm. "I so admired 'The Onyx Vase.' It was so—evocative."

Lady Clarke, whom Michael last recalled seeing in the drawing room of Mrs. Chase's Seminary, slid up to them in a flurry of orange silk and fragrant plumes. "I am still partial to 'Alas, fair cruelty,' myself," she said, with a secretive little smile.

Lady Portman moved closer to him, tightening her clasp on his arm. She gave a glare to the other women surrounding them. "Right now, though, Lord Morley, let me introduce you to some of the other guests. So many of them are literary-minded, and are so eager to greet you."

She led him farther into the crowded ballroom, while Lady Clarke stared after them with smoldering dark eyes. In truth, Michael was rather glad to be borne away from the woman. She was becomingly annoyingly persistent of late, sending heavily scented missives to his lodgings. Ever since he had begun to break the rules, in fact.

He stopped to speak to various acquaintances, to talk of other balls, routs, plays, and exchange *on dits* about people who were not here. As Lady Portman and her circle spoke of a certain Madame Varens who was performing at Drury Lane, Michael took a glass of champagne from a passing footman's tray and gazed about him at the throngs of people.

As he was taller than most of the crowd, he could see over the ocean of dancers, the sea of potted palms. Near the invitingly half-open French doors was another knot of people, much like the group that had greeted him on his arrival, with one great difference.

Most of this gathering were men, and they clustered about two tall, redheaded women.

One of them had her back to him, but the one who faced him he recognized as the Duchess of Wayland, and he immediately understood the draw for those men. The Duchess of Wayland, nee Mrs. Georgina Beaumont, was a vivid beauty, a famous artist in her own right, and, since her exalted marriage, a leader of Society. Michael had talked with her about art and writing before, and liked her very much, even though he had been oddly unmoved by the renowned "green fire" of her eyes. Tonight, she was like a brilliant, exotic bird of paradise amid pastel sparrows with her bright blue gown and sparkling sapphires.

The woman who was turned away from Michael looked as if she could prove to be no less beautiful, even if she was less colorful. Her hair, a river of red ringlets, was piled atop her head and anchored with a bandeau of pale sea green silk twisted with seed pearls. Her tall, slender figure was set off perfectly by a gown of pale green satin that just barely skimmed her waist and the long length of her legs. She tilted her swanlike neck as one of her companions spoke to her, and one long curl slid over her shoulder.

Michael was drawn to her, this mysterious, sea-clad woman. She seemed an oasis of serenity in the over-crowded ballroom, a poised, elegant, gardenia-like blossom that promised sanctuary from all the empty chatter, the high-pitched laughter, the hands pulling at his arms.

He murmured some excuse to Lady Portman, and made his way across the room, drawn by the woman in green. It was not an easy endeavor; he was stopped numerous times, obliged to make polite conversation. Yet finally he was able to break free, to skirt around the edge of the dance floor. He was very nearly to the crowd by the French doors, when the woman turned.

Michael almost dropped his champagne glass. Standing not fifteen feet away from him in the Port-

man ballroom, clad in that shimmering satin and
pearls, was—Mrs. Chase.

For one off-guard instant, he was filled with a deep
flush of pleasure—pleasure at seeing her again, when
she had been so much in his mind of late. And she
was more beautiful than he remembered, her hair a
glory when released from those hideous caps.

Pleasure was quickly swept away by cold shock, and
Michael impatiently shook his head, certain he was
hallucinating. Mrs. Chase could not be here. He must
be dreaming, hallucinating.

He closed his eyes quickly, and opened them again.
She was still there, and she was undoubtedly Mrs.
Chase. She was watching him, her head tilted quizzi-
cally as if she could not believe *he* was there, either.

Then her gaze narrowed, and her lips pinched
together.

Yes. It was assuredly Mrs. Chase. Michael pushed
away his bemusement, and pasted on a wry half-smile.
He could do nothing but go forward. "Mrs. Chase,"
he murmured to himself. "Fancy meeting you here."

Whatever was she doing here?

Rosalind stared around her at the teeming ballroom.
Once, long ago, when she had been a young girl, she
had daydreamed about such scenes. Had imagined
herself in beautiful gowns, surrounded by handsome
swains who flattered her and flirted with her.

The tableau she found herself in now was indeed
very close to those old dreams. Her sea green gown
was exquisite, and there were more handsome gentlemen than she could count. When she first stepped into
the ballroom at Georgina's side, she had felt giddy,
dizzy, almost overcome by the color and noise of it
all—so very different from her daily life.

But too much time had passed since her girlhood
dreams; too much had happened. The dreamy daughter of the local vicar had grown up, married, been
widowed, struggled to build up her own school. She
was no longer as starry-eyed as she had once been.

She saw this crowd for what it was, a seething cauldron of gossip and decadence beneath a veneer of frothy glamour. For a brief while, though, rules—*her* rules—had held them in check, at least outwardly.

She was not here to make merry, she reminded herself. She was here merely to discover what had made the popularity of *A Lady's Rules* wane, and to set things right. When she had done that, she would leave her borrowed finery behind and return to the quiet life of the Seminary.

That was truly all she wanted. *Truly,* she told herself, even as she sipped at the sinfully delicious champagne and listened to Georgina relate a scandalous *on dit* to her gathered friends. London life had no interest for Rosalind, really it did not.

She told herself this even as she scanned a gaze over the dancers, trying to detect any infraction of the rules that could be causing diminished sales. She saw nothing there—everyone was wearing gloves, and holding their partners at the prescribed distance. When she had first entered the Portman mansion, she had noticed one or two tiny things—a couple laughing too loudly, a man who had had a bit too much to drink—but nothing to give any alarm.

She had not yet seen Lord Morley or any of his cronies, though. That might explain all the good behavior this evening.

"May I fetch you another glass of champagne, Mrs. Chase?" the gentleman beside her asked.

Rosalind looked down with surprise to see that her crystal flute was empty. However had that happened? She *never* overimbibed. Then she noticed that she was indeed a bit light-headed. "Oh, no, thank you," she answered, with a small measure of regret. It *was* very good champagne. "Perhaps a lemonade, though."

"Of course! I shall return forthwith."

Rosalind wasn't sure he *could* return "forthwith" in such a crush, but she smiled at him gratefully, and half-turned to watch him thread his way through the crowd. She handed her empty glass to a footman, and resumed her inspection of the dancers and the crowds that clustered about the edges of the room.

Her gaze skimmed over a couple strolling arm in arm; a group of young misses, one of whom was Georgina's sister-in-law Lady Emily; a tall gentleman in a midnight blue velvet coat . . .

Her gaze veered back to that gentleman. As she saw who it was, she knew he could surely not be called a "gentleman"—gentlemen did not go about trying to ruin ladies' livelihoods! They did not flaunt themselves and their so-called poetry, as Lord Morley did.

And it was Lord Morley who stood only a few feet away from her, watching her as if he had never seen her before in his life. Almost as if—as if he *admired* her.

But that could not be. She was not some dashing, daring titled lady, the sort who Georgina said clustered about him. Perhaps he meant to mock her, then, by watching her so intently. To poke fun at her for being in a ballroom where she so obviously did not belong.

She frowned at the thought, and her head gave a warning pang. She started to turn away from the sight of him, to try to immerse herself again in Georgina's conversation, but she stopped when she saw Lady Clarke come to Lord Morley's side.

As Rosalind watched, Lady Clarke, the mother of one of Rosalind's very own pupils, laid her hand on Lord Morley's arm and stepped up close to him. Far too close for propriety. Lady Clarke went up on tiptoe and whispered into his ear, her ample white bosom displayed in a tiny orange silk bodice. Lord Morley placed his hand—his *ungloved* hand—on her waist. It was unclear if he was pushing her away or holding her there.

Rosalind found she could scarcely tear her gaze away from the ridiculous spectacle. But when she finally managed to look elsewhere, she saw that the people around them, far from being aghast, watched with smirks and smiles of scandalized satisfaction. No one cared at all that Lord Morley was breaking at least four—no, five!—rules.

Much to Rosalind's shock, however, she found that it was not entirely the rule-breaking that pained her. She also felt a sharp pang of something that felt suspiciously like jealousy in her heart.

Her head throbbed in earnest as she watched Lord Morley's hand slide from Lady Clarke's waist to her arm. He said something quietly to her, and her red lips curved up in an enticing smile. Lady Clarke began to turn away from him, but Rosalind turned first, unable to bear the disgusting sight a moment longer.

She needed to be alone. The noise of the ballroom had risen to an infernal din, and even the orchestra was too loud and clanging.

"Do excuse me for a moment," she murmured to Georgina. "I must go to the ladies' withdrawing room."

Georgina's emerald eyes, so bright and laughing only an instant before, turned dark with concern. She laid her hand on Rosalind's arm, her sapphire bracelets tinkling. "Is something amiss, Rosalind? Shall I come with you?"

Rosalind managed to give her a smile. "It is a slight headache only. I think I just need a quiet moment. You must stay here and enjoy the party, keep an eye on Emily. She is such a sought-after young lady."

"Are you certain? I can make Alex leave his discussion of new farming techniques and watch his sister while I am gone. My husband needs to remember his social duties anyway! He *is* a duke, after all, even if he would rather just be a gentleman farmer!" Georgina laughed, but the soft glow on her face spoke volumes of her love for her "gentleman farmer."

Rosalind felt another twist of envy, and she did not like it at all. How *could* she be envious of anyone, least of all Georgie, who so richly deserved her happiness? Or of Lady Clarke, whose impropriety was legendary? To be envious at all was horribly unladylike.

It was *not* envy, Rosalind told herself. It was simply fatigue. She was not accustomed to the social whirl.

"Oh, no," she said. "Leave His Grace to his conversation. I will just go sit down for a moment and will be quite well soon."

She gave Georgina what she hoped was a reassuring smile, and turned to make her way through the ballroom. Since she was of little importance in the grand *ton* scheme of things, it did not take her very long to make her escape—no one stopped her to talk, aside from one or two of Georgina's friends. She slipped out the ballroom doors and past the butler, who waited to announce any latecomers.

The ladies' withdrawing room was down the staircase from the grand ballroom, and along a quiet, dim corridor. The long expanse was lit only by a couple of branches of candelabra, and only the faintest echo of music and voices could be heard from the party.

Already Rosalind could feel the tight band of her headache loosening. She leaned back for a moment against the papered wall, and closed her eyes.

So it is true, she thought. Lord Morley *was* the one responsible for the diminished popularity of the rules. He was using his dash, his reputation as a rogue and a poet, to break the rules of good conduct, and others were following him. Not just young nodcocks like her brother, either, but people in polite society.

She did not know why she should feel such a sourness of disappointment at the realization. Surely she had known all along. Yet it was one thing to know; it was another to *know,* to see it with her own eyes.

Morley *was* a care-for-nothing, a slapdash poet who squandered the benefits and duties of his high position. She had always known that. And yet—and yet, he had been so kind to her that day in her office. He had brought her tea, had made her laugh.

She could scarcely reconcile that man with the one who had stood so intimately with Lady Clarke in the ballroom.

She was such a fool to feel so disappointed.

As Rosalind reached up to rub at her temples, a voice came echoing down the empty corridor.

"Good evening, Mrs. Chase. What an unexpected pleasure it is to see you here."

Lord Morley. Rosalind's eyes flew open, and she turned to see him standing there, half in the shadows. He looked mysterious, almost insubstantial, with a single flickering beam of candlelight falling over his dark hair, his high cheekbones. She could almost have fancied that he was a ghost, the spirit of a wild pirate of old, come back to claim his treasure—his woman.

Unfortunately, he was all too real. And he had caught her yet again at her most vulnerable.

Drat the man.

Chapter Nine

"A gentleman must never approach a lady uninvited at a soiree."

~~A Lady's Rules for Proper Behavior,~~ Chapter Five

*R*osalind pushed herself away from the wall, staring dazedly at Lord Morley. She knew she was gaping like the veriest lackwit, but she could not seem to help herself. He was like a mirage—or a nightmare—standing there in the shadowed, quiet corridor. She had known she would see him here in London sooner or later; that was really one of the purposes of her visit, was it not? To somehow stop him from his rule-breaking.

The difficulty was, her plan was only half conceived, and she had no clue what to do with him now. She had not thought beyond arriving in Town, and doing *something* to save her situation. What, she was not sure, but she had imagined that a plan would occur to her once she saw Lord Morley.

She had not imagined she would meet him like *this,* however. Alone, in the half-dark. She thought herself a self-possessed woman, a woman of social poise. Of good sense. All that sense had fled, though, and she did not know what to say.

She straightened her shoulders, and reached up to be sure her hair was smooth. "Good evening, Lord Morley. I did not see you standing there."

"No. I can see that." He moved closer to her still

in the shadows. The gold threads embroidered on his cream-colored waistcoat glinted in the candlelight. "I did not mean to startle you."

"Indeed? Then what are you doing here, Lord Morley, lurking in the shadows? I was under the impression that this was the direction to the ladies' withdrawing room." Or perhaps she had taken a wrong turn? There appeared to be no one about in this part of the house at all. Rosalind tried to draw in a deep breath, but her chest felt tight, constricted—and not from her light stays or silk chemise. It was from this man's very presence. He made her feel unsure; he seemed to take up all the air in the narrow corridor.

It was just because she loathed him, she told herself sternly. Because he was a wastrel, who squandered his life in shallow, careless ways.

That was all it was. That was the only reason she felt her face burn, her fingertips and toes turn icy. She just wanted to be out of his presence.

"I believe the withdrawing room is the other way," he answered lightly, with a shrug of his wide, velvet-covered shoulders. "Yet I could not believe my eyes when I saw you in the ballroom. You are one of the last people I would expect to see here. I had to assure myself that it was you, Mrs. Chase."

He could not believe it because she was of such lowly station, perhaps? Rosalind frowned. She would have thought that men who flouted their position by writing poetry would not think of such things. But then, he *was* of the *ton*—she should not be amazed that he was like everyone else. She remembered the shifting of peoples' gazes, the smirks, when they discovered she owned a school.

She was past caring about all that now. She had always done what she had to do, to take care of herself and her family. Why, then, did it sting so when *he* implied as much?

"Oh, Lord Morley?" she said, with a forced, careless little laugh. At least, she hoped it sounded careless. "And why is that? Because I am a mere schoolmistress?"

He gave her a smile, a knowing grin that made her cheeks burn hotter. "Not at all. Because it seems as if Town would be too wicked for you, Mrs. Chase. Too full of temptations. Sins."

Temptations? Such as a pair of fathomless dark eyes that seemed to see into her very soul? A heady whiff of some citrus soap? Oh, yes. Apparently Town, or at least Lady Portman's corridor, was full of those. She stepped back from him, until she felt the edge of a marble-topped table against her hips.

He just took another step toward her, so close she could see the faint blue-black shadow of whiskers along his jawline.

"It is not safe here, Mrs. Chase," he said softly, tauntingly. "Not like it is behind the high walls of your school."

Rosalind's gaze flickered past him to the painting on the wall, but she still sensed him there. Sensed his warmth. She did not see the indifferent seascape at all. "Ah, but Town has become much more civilized of late, has it not? Since people have found a source of manners, of good behavior."

"You mean *A Lady's Rules,* do you not?" he said, with a rich chuckle. That sound seemed to vibrate deep inside of her. "Do you truly think of them as a simple guide to manners? A gentle suggestion of how to be—civilized?"

She looked back to him, unable to break her gaze away from the velvet of his eyes. He watched her intently, leaning toward her, as if he truly cared about her answer. "Of course. What else could they be?"

"Oh, now, I do not know. A way to keep people in line? To make them conform to someone else's views of how things should be?" He leaned one hand against the wall, carelessly, as if he was not aware of his action. The soft fabric of his sleeve was near—so near— her neck, her bare shoulder.

"C-conform?" she choked out. She tried to edge away from his arm, but the table blocked her path. "Conform to what?"

"Society has always been constrictive in certain ways," he said. "Yet there has also been room for a degree of freedom for people who, shall we say, have a different way of looking at things."

"People such as you, perhaps?" she asked. "People who behave in wild ways, not caring what boundaries they cross, or who they hurt by it."

Something flickered in the sherry brown depths of his eyes, a flash of anger or maybe even pain. But it was gone in an instant, and he glanced away from her with a laugh. "I would never knowingly hurt anyone, Mrs. Chase. I only try to enjoy my life; it is far too short to do otherwise. How can that harm people?"

Rosalind didn't know what he was saying, what he meant. Her head was spinning, her ears ringing. She wanted to move away from him, to run away, but she was frozen to the spot. "How have the rules hurt anyone?" she cried, more passionately than she intended. Her voice echoed along the corridor.

He seemed startled by her vehemence, and studied her closer. His hand, as of its own volition, moved to her hair, to the long curl that lay along her neck. It twined like a twist of red silk around his finger.

Rosalind forgot to breathe. She could not move away, she could not do anything but stare at her hair twined about his long, elegant finger.

"Oh, Mrs. Chase," he whispered. "They hurt people in ways far too complicated for me to explain. They are hurting *you,* if you could only see it."

Hurting her? *No!* They were the only thing that was saving her—the only thing that could begin to help her brother. *Morley* was the one who was hurting her. She had left the safety of her school to come here and stop him.

But it was hard, indeed almost impossible, to remember that now. She reached up to grasp his wrist, to push him away, but she could not seem to. Her fingers curled around his velvet cuff, and she leaned closer to him . . .

"Well, well," a voice said. "What is all this?"

Rosalind jerked away, as if she was burned, and almost tripped over the table. As she righted herself, clinging to the cold marble, a hot, red rush of shame flooded through her. What was she doing, standing here in the dark, practically *embracing* Lord Morley? Morley, of all people! She had broken at least six— no, seven—of her own rules in just those few seconds.

Moon madness. That was the only explanation. Or perhaps the spell of the city, the unfamiliar social whirl, that made her lose her head. Made her forget what was truly important.

She peered down the corridor to see Georgina standing there, her famous sapphires glittering like a blue fire in the candlelight. Georgina watched her with no hint of condemnation—that would never be Georgina's way. There was speculation in her eyes, and a hint of amusement.

That amusement was almost worse than condemnation. It was like a splash of icy water, bringing her back into reality. Rosalind slipped past Lord Morley and hurried down the corridor toward her friend.

"Georgina," she said, and was dismayed to hear the breathlessness of her voice. "I was just—just coming to find you."

"Oh, yes? I trust your headache is better." Georgina's gaze shifted past Rosalind to Lord Morley, who had moved away from the wall and stood in a flickering beam of candlelight. "Viscount Morley, is it not?"

"Indeed it is, Duchess." Aside from a faint thickness in his tone, there was absolutely no change in his demeanor. It was as if he was completely unaffected by their brief, strange, unsettling scene. He pushed the waves of his dark hair back from his brow, and came forward to bow over Georgina's hand.

"I was not aware you knew my friend Mrs. Chase,"

she said, tilting her head as she looked up at him speculatively.

"My sister attends her excellent Seminary," he answered, and glanced over at Rosalind. There was a plea in his eyes—perhaps an apology?

But Rosalind could not bring herself to look directly at him just yet. She could scarcely even think.

"Lady Violet, yes," said Georgina. "I have met her. She is a lovely girl. My friend's school obviously agrees with her. No doubt you were chatting about her education just now?"

"Among other things," Lord Morley murmured.

"*Fascinating* things, I am sure," Georgina said. "I would love to stay here and chat with the two of you, but I fear we have no time for that at the moment. Rosalind, I came to find you to tell you there is something in the ballroom you *must* see."

Something in the ballroom she had to see? Rosalind could not imagine what it could possibly be. More dancers? More gossiping dowagers? But she found she longed for the crowded ballroom, for the noise and distraction of it. At least there Georgina could not question her about this scene, as Rosalind could see her friend longed to do. There, she could not think about all this nonsense.

That could wait for tonight, when she was alone in the quiet opulence of Georgina's finest guest bedchamber.

"Of course," she said. "I will come at once."

"Good. Though I fear you will not be at all happy when you see it." Georgina took Rosalind's hand and started to turn away, back to the staircase to the ballroom. Then she glanced back at Morley. "Lord Morley, we would be happy to have you call at our house at any time that is convenient. My husband and I so enjoyed your last volume of poems."

Lord Morley bowed. "That is very kind of you, Your Grace. Thank you."

Georgina nodded, and drew Rosalind along with her up the stairs.

"Why did you invite that man to your house, Georgina?" Rosalind whispered.

Georgina turned to her, auburn brows arched in surprise. "I thought you liked him, Rosie! Why else would you be standing there alone with him? He *is* very handsome."

Rosalind just shook her head. She had no words, not right now. The usually unflappable Mrs. Chase was—flapped. She felt like an unsure young girl, not like the thirty-year-old widow she was.

"We must speak more of this later," Georgina said, as they reached the closed ballroom doors. There was a strange rumbling noise from behind those inlaid panels, a crash, a roar. "But for now, my dear—you must brace yourself."

Blast! What was he thinking of?

Michael turned away as Mrs. Chase and the duchess hurried off, and closed his eyes to suck in a large breath of air. It did no good, though—the corridor was still filled with the fresh, green scent of her perfume.

He braced his fists against the wall, and restrained the fierce impulse to drive them through the painted silk paper.

He knew what he had been thinking of. He had been thinking of Mrs. Chase's bright curls, her white skin above the silken line of her bodice. The look in her blue eyes as she watched him. Once he had thought of them as ice. But tonight, they glowed as brilliant as starlight.

Brilliant with dislike, mayhap? Or a deep, hidden desire? The same desire that sparked inside him when her hair curled about his finger. As he looked at that one red curl, he had envisioned the wealth of her hair spread over her shoulders, over his chest and arms, the whiteness of linen pillows . . .

He pounded against the wall, until a painting hanging above him rattled perilously. He had been having those lustful thoughts about Mrs. Chase! *Mrs. Chase,* of all people. The woman who wore ugly caps, and trumpeted the rules to all and sundry. She would not know a free moment, a spontaneous act, if they reached up and snatched one of those caps off her head.

And yet she was beautiful tonight, in her fashionable gown, her chic coiffure. She almost appeared like a normal female. Yet what he had forgotten was that beneath that pale green satin beat the heart of a true rule-follower.

But she had not been thinking of the rules when they stood there, so close together in the near darkness. And neither had he, despite their words to each other about manners and etiquette. He had thought only of tasting her kiss, breathing in the scent of her.

Her lips were surprisingly lush and pink when not pinched together disapprovingly. Her eyes were wide and wondering, so young for just that moment.

There was more to her than what she showed the world. She went to great pains to appear cool, prim, proper, always so very in control. And she was quite successful—even he had seen only that façade. Now he suspected there was something else, something hidden there. Perhaps so hidden that not even she herself could see it.

And *that* was what drew him to her, he realized. He wanted to discover her hidden heart, the free soul she buried beneath her manners and her ugly gowns. He had glimpsed her for the merest instant tonight, he had even held her, felt the trembling inside of her.

Then she was snatched away, and he had watched the veil of her propriety fall over her again. There was a hectic red flush on her fair cheeks, the freckles she tried to hide standing out in golden relief. She would not even look at him, and seemed appalled at her friend's invitation to him to call.

It was deeply saddening to see. He wanted to go after her, to catch her in his arms and *demand* that she give him back the woman he had seen so fleetingly. But he had not, of course. That would only have driven Mrs. Chase further away, made her retreat deeper beneath her careful façade.

Now that he had glimpsed her inner secrets, he wanted to know more of her. He *had* to know.

He would accept the Duchess of Wayland's invitation to call. Very soon, before Mrs. Chase had time to scurry back behind the high walls of her school.

Perhaps he would even go tomorrow.

Michael pushed himself away from the wall, and straightened his coat and his cravat (not pink tonight, but sky blue—much like Mrs. Chase's eyes). As he turned away, he glimpsed a flash of something pale against the dark carpet runner. He bent down and picked up a fan. A pale green satin fan, edged in white lace and scattered with tiny, glittering beads.

Mrs. Chase's fan. She must have dropped it when they were standing here together. The soft pleats still smelled of her perfume.

Michael tucked it inside his coat. Now he had the perfect excuse to call at the Wayland house, if the duchess's invitation was not enough.

With a smile, he strolled to the staircase leading to the ballroom. Halfway up, he became aware of an odd noise from the party, a rush of wild laughter, a crash, a shriek. He hurried his steps, along with the other stragglers from the ball who lingered on the stairs—and stopped abruptly in the doorway.

He could scarcely believe what he was seeing!

Chapter Ten

"When dancing, a proper distance must be kept between partners at all times."
A Lady's Rules for Proper Behavior, Chapter Three

Rosalind could hardly believe what she was seeing. The ball was not quite the crush it had been when Rosalind left; no doubt many people had gone on to other soirees or home to their beds. But there were many people remaining, and several of them—nay, most of them—were riveted on one spectacle.

Rosalind froze as she stepped into the ballroom. This could not be happening. This was just a nightmare. Obviously, she had not yet awakened from her dream-scene in the corridor with Lord Morley. Her face, her hands, her whole being froze with the hot-icy feel of sheer humiliation.

Sprawled out flat in the middle of the parquet dance floor was Allen, dressed in a most outlandish Pierrot costume. The loose black and white satin of his baggy pantaloons and tunic spread about him in a shimmering puddle, and his black velvet cap fell drunkenly over his eyes. He slowly sat up, pushing the cap back, and the observers gathered in a ring around him stepped back—all but a large, buxom matron in purple satin, who menaced Allen with her reticule, and a petite, sobbing miss.

Laughter and titters rose as an inexorable tidal wave

through the crowd, audible even over the lovely music that still played.

Rosalind rubbed her gloved hand over her eyes, but it did not make the surreal scene disappear. Another young man, whom Rosalind did not know, went to help haul Allen to his feet. This man, too, wore a costume, the garb of a Roman centurion with a clanking brass breastplate.

She turned to Georgina, who was trying, not very successfully, to hide her smile behind her fan.

"What happened here?" Rosalind demanded.

Georgina lowered her fan, and used it to tap thoughtfully at her chin. "I am afraid I could not say exactly. I was over there, talking with some friends, when we became aware of some, er, disturbance. People running about, girls shrieking. Then—this." Her voice ended on a tiny hiccup that sounded suspiciously like a giggle.

Rosalind sighed. She could not really blame Georgina for laughing. It *did* look so oddly comical. Yet, somehow, she could not quite laugh herself. Not with her cheeks burning and her head pounding. There was probably no chance she could just pretend not to know Allen. Everyone in the *ton* knew everything about everyone else—even such insignificant sprigs as Allen and Rosalind.

As Rosalind turned and prepared to wade into the fray, Georgina's sister-in-law Emily rushed up to them. Her china blue eyes sparkled with excitement. She was in her third Season now, but had obviously never seen anything like *this* at the many, many balls she attended!

"Oh, Georgie!" she cried. "Isn't it just too funny? And I was right there when it happened!" Then her gaze fell on Rosalind, and some of the sparkle faded. "I'm sorry, Mrs. Chase. I did forget that Mr. Lucas is your brother."

"That is quite all right, Lady Emily," Rosalind said. "But what exactly *did* happen here?"

Emily glanced back over to Pierrot and the Roman,

who had now been joined by Louis XIV in powdered wig and high-heeled shoes. The matron in purple still shouted incoherently at them, and swiped at Allen with her beaded reticule. "Well, I was dancing with Mr. Elliott, and we were very near Miss Anderson and her partner, Lord St. Regis. Miss Anderson is Lady Anderson's daughter, you know." Emily gestured toward the matron and the sobbing young lady hidden in her shadow. "It was all quite ordinary. Then, all of a sudden, Miss Anderson screamed! And Lord St. Regis hit poor Mr. Lucas."

Rosalind was completely bewildered. "But what was Allen doing here at all? He was not invited to this ball, and even if he was this is *not* a fancy-dress event." The cabbage-head was not even supposed to be in London, but hard at his studies at Cambridge.

"I do not know," Emily said. "Miss Anderson was saying he just grabbed her and kissed her! And when he was on the floor, having been planted a facer by Lord St. Regis, Lady Anderson came up and hit him with her reticule. I have heard that she carries a very large vinaigrette in that reticule." She lowered her voice confidingly, and added, "I do believe, Mrs. Chase, that Mr. Lucas is quite foxed. He smelled rather—pungent."

Foxed. Oh, wonderful. That was just what this situation required. Not just an idiot, but a drunken idiot.

"Thank you for that information, Lady Emily," Rosalind said. Her tone was surprisingly calm, considering the roiling turmoil in her heart. She curled her hands into fists, and marched across the ballroom, Georgina and Emily hurrying behind her.

Fortunately, before they reached the violent scene Georgina's husband, Alexander, the Duke of Wayland, joined them. He had apparently just returned from his farming conversation, and seen his wife and sister being drawn into a scandalous scene. He took Georgina's arm, and whispered, "What have you done now, Georgie?"

Georgina looked at him indignantly. "Why do you

assume that just because there is a disturbance *I* had something to do with it?"

He grinned at her. "Because, my love, you usually do."

She laughed. "Well, I did naught to cause it this time. It is poor Rosie's brother."

Alexander looked to Allen, and his handsome face darkened as Lady Anderson landed another blow on Allen's head. "So I see. Well, ladies, shall we discover what can be done?"

The gathered crowd parted for the duke and duchess, allowing them to walk unimpeded to Allen's side. As Alexander spoke quietly to the red-faced Lady Anderson, Rosalind turned to her brother.

Do not hit him, she told herself sternly. *Be calm. Remember the rules. Surely there is one about not pummeling gentlemen in public places.* Even foolish younger brothers.

"Rosie!" Allen cried. For one instant, relief flashed across his face. Perhaps, Rosalind thought, he supposed his big sister had come yet again to his rescue. But the relief was quickly replaced by chagrin, and then bluster. "What the deuce are you doing here?"

"What am *I* doing here?" Rosalind said, trying to keep her voice quiet. She was all too aware of the many people watching them with avid interest—including parents of some of her pupils. "*You* are meant to be at university, not gallivanting about London making an absolute fool of yourself—and of me."

"Ah, Rosie, you are making too much of it," Allen insisted. He sighed, releasing a wave of that "pungent" odor Lady Emily had mentioned. He pulled off his battered cap and twisted it between his hands. "It is nothing. A mere wager."

"A *what*?" Rosalind's voice rose dangerously as she felt her temper slipping out of her control. She felt a soft touch on her arm, and glanced over to see Georgina's reassuring smile.

"Lady Portman says we may speak privately in her library," Georgina said. "Perhaps that would be better than staying here? Alex and Emily will smooth things over with the others."

Rosalind turned to Alexander. Indeed, he had already smoothed the ruffled purple feathers of Lady Anderson and her sobbing daughter. The indignant matron was even smiling, and much of the crowd was wandering away as the spectacle faded.

"Ah, young men," Alexander said to the general gathering, with a handsome, rueful smile. "What can one do?"

There was a knowing ripple of laughter, and Rosalind began to think—to hope—that all might not be lost after all. A faint ray of relief pierced the gloom of her anger and humiliation. But it did not entirely eradicate them—they still simmered in the depths of her mind.

She and Allen would not always have a duke to rescue them, and Allen had to come to understand that. Even if he understood so little else—like how precarious their livelihood was at the moment. She had this bank loan to pay, and not enough to pay it. The money from *A Lady's Rules* that she had counted on was dwindling away. If pupils abandoned her school due to a scandal attached to her family, she and Allen would be entirely lost.

"Yes," she said to Georgina. "We should retire to the library." Then, not giving Allen a chance to argue, Rosalind took one of his arms and Georgina the other, and they marched him out of the ballroom. Behind them, the music resumed, and Alexander led Lady Anderson into the dance.

Rosalind was still not entirely certain what had just happened here, but she was quite sure it had *something* to do with Lord Morley.

When Michael returned to the ballroom, many of the guests had departed. But there were still a great many people dancing, sitting in the white brocade chairs lining the dance floor, and taking turns about the room. Everything appeared just as a ball ought to—except for the two men huddled in the shadows by the door.

Mr. Gilmore and Lord Carteret, dressed incongruously as a Roman centurion and a fop from the last century.

"Morley!" Gilmore cried, his voice hoarse with relief. "You are here."

"Yes," Michael answered, as they pulled him into the shadows with them. "I am here. What, though, are *you* two doing here? And dressed like that?"

"It is that wager," Carteret said, flicking at the deep lace of his cuff. "We thought Lucas would see he cannot win if we brought him here tonight. So we made a sort of secondary wager."

Carteret seemed faintly amused by the whole thing, while Gilmore looked pale and shaken. Michael glanced from one to the other of them, a strange, sick feeling growing in his stomach. Something had obviously happened while he was lingering with Mrs. Chase in the dark corridor, something involving that very lady's brother.

Something else she could hate him for. Because he knew, deep down, that she would surely blame him for whatever trouble young Lucas had wreaked tonight.

He swept a quick glance over the ballroom, and did not see Mrs. Chase, Mr. Lucas, or the Duchess of Wayland anywhere. Lady Emily, though, stood not very far away, watching their little group with far too much shrewdness for such a young miss. Michael gave her a rakish grin, hoping she would blush and turn away. She just laughed, but she *did* leave, crossing the room to her brother's side. The duke was talking with a very buxom lady in bright purple satin, whom Michael recognized as Lady Anderson, mother of the prettiest debutante this Season.

Michael turned back to Gilmore and Carteret. "Now tell me exactly why you three came here in costume."

Carteret gave him a resentful scowl. "You are not our father, Morley, to be taking us to task."

"Carteret . . ." Gilmore said nervously.

"But," Carteret continued, "since you *are* our friend, we will tell you. We were at a masquerade at Vauxhall, with the loveliest little bits o'muslin you ever saw. There was a bit too much wine and brandy, too, and so we conceived the idea of coming here."

Michael stared at them through narrowed eyes. "That cannot be the entire story."

"It is *almost* the entire story!" Gilmore said. "Except that Carteret dared Lucas to steal a kiss from Miss Anderson, then dash away before he was caught. Miss Anderson is the Diamond of the Season, y'know."

"It would have worked, too, if the chit hadn't sent up such a fuss," said Carteret. "Then Lord St. Regis and Miss Anderson's mama laid Lucas low."

Miss Anderson "sending up a fuss" was surely exactly what Carteret had been hoping for, Michael thought. Public humiliation was probably the only way Lucas was going to be persuaded he must follow the rules, and thus allow Carteret to win the silly wager. "Where is Lucas now?"

"His dragon sister and the Duchess of Wayland marched him out of here, quite smartishly," said Gilmore. "And the duke calmed everyone down in here. Even Lady Anderson."

"So you see?" Carteret said languidly. "There was no harm done."

No harm done? Could these—these *loobies* truly be so very ignorant? Their prank had very nearly humiliated a young man and ruined his sister's business. Michael knew very well how unforgiving people in Society could be if they felt they had been embarrassed, and these boys' escapade had involved the loveliest debutante in London and her snobbish parents. Only the intervention of people as influential as the Waylands had saved the entire ridiculous situation. And now this smirking bacon-brain was prating about no harm done.

Michael could not stop himself from reaching out

to grab Carteret by the lace of his cascading jabot—his anger blinded him, burned white-hot behind his eyes. Carteret's eyes widened in shock, and he made ineffectual little jabs with his beringed hands as Gilmore, looking on, gave an incoherent cry.

"Don't you realize what could have happened here tonight? Lucas's *sister* was here. Her reputation was at risk as well as his, if your 'harmless' prank had not ended where it did. The Waylands saved all of your hides this time, but next time you will not be so fortunate, you brainless pups."

Carteret's face was turning red beneath his layer of rice powder, and his hands clawed ever more insistently at Michael's arm. Michael loosened his grip, but still held onto the lace.

"You were the one who claimed we could break all the rules and still be accepted," Carteret gasped. "Are you so quick to change your mind, just because Lucas got taken to task?"

Michael had never meant his words like *this*. Yes, following all of *A Lady's Rules* was absurd, was soul-killing. But their behavior this evening, that of all three of them, had been beyond the pale. Michael himself would never do anything so rash, so ill thought out. He would never actually damage anyone.

Would he? Certain youthful indiscretions flashed through his mind, pranks every bit as ridiculous as the one this trio had tried tonight. Yet that had been long ago; he had learned from those mistakes, as one day these boys would have to learn from theirs. That sort of wild, pointless rule-breaking was far behind Michael.

Then another vision flowed through his mind—himself, pulling Lady Clarke close to him and putting his arm about her waist. All in this very ballroom, not three hours ago—and under the gaze of Mrs. Chase.

A heat that felt uncomfortably more like regret than his previous anger flowed through his veins. He released Carteret, who fell back a step and reached up to rub at his throat.

"You are far more dangerous than we are, Morley," Carteret said weakly. "People pay far more attention to *your* infractions than they ever would to ours. And I think the ladies over there would agree with me."

Michael, still trembling with the force of his anger and uncertainty, glanced back over his shoulder.

Mrs. Chase and the Duchess of Wayland stood in the doorway of the ballroom, with Allen Lucas nowhere in evidence. The duchess paid them no attention; her gaze was scanning over the crowd, no doubt looking for her husband.

But Mrs. Chase was staring right at them—at *him*. Her posture was perfectly straight, her expression completely composed. Her eyes, though, burned with a freezing, pale blue light, even more vivid than the duchess's sapphires. She watched him, unblinking, for a long, still moment, the force of her disdain clear. She then slowly turned her back to him and moved away into the sea of people.

It was as if their moment in the corridor had never happened at all. As if he had never glimpsed the heat that lay beneath her serene, proper exterior.

He felt as if he had just lost something precious, something he had not even realized he could desire so much until this very moment—something as beautiful as Mrs. Chase's smile.

He had the strongest urge to rush after her, to apologize, to beg for her understanding. He could not, though. It would do no good, not when her eyes were as cold as they were right now. She had drawn back into herself, after shyly peering forth when they were alone. She was again the self-contained Mrs. Chase. And how could he ask her to understand something he could not yet understand himself?

He should talk to her, and he would. But not here. Not now, with all these people about. He strode away from Gilmore and Carteret, down the staircase toward the Portman's front door. He reached inside his coat and touched the satin and lace fan—Mrs. Chase's fan. Tomorrow, he would take it to her, would talk to her.

Surely by then he would know what to say. Words were his profession, after all—he ought to be able to find the right ones.

He was not sure why he felt he had to speak to her so urgently. She was a woman who stood for everything he so disliked, had so strained against all his life. He only knew he *did* have to talk to her, to see her again. He had to find the woman he had met in the corridor.

Chapter Eleven

"Be very careful whom you choose to confide in—be certain they are true friends."
A Lady's Rules for Proper Behavior, Chapter Ten

"*G*ood heavens, what an evening!" Georgina collapsed onto a settee in her own sitting room, and kicked off her satin slippers before propping her feet on a low footstool. "I cannot recall a more diverting soiree, can you, Emily?"

"Not at all," Emily replied, settling herself in an armchair. "There was that jug-bitten young man who tried to slide down the banister at the Eversleys' ball last Season, but I would say . . ." She broke off, and cast a guilty smile in Rosalind's direction. "Not that I enjoyed seeing *your* brother get into trouble, Mrs. Chase."

Rosalind gave her a small smile in return. A small one was all she could manage, she was so very tired. She wished she could kick off her shoes like Georgina, but it did not seem proper. Not in front of people. "It is quite all right, Lady Emily. Allen *did* look ridiculous there, and it was entirely his own fault." His—and Lord Morley's, for encouraging such silliness among impressionable young men. "I wonder if I should go up and see how he fares?"

"Oh, no, Rosie," Georgina said, scratching the ears of her spoiled white terrier Lady Kate. "Alex will have him tucked away in a trice. He knows exactly how to deal with drunk young men, after all his years in the army."

"It was very kind of you to give him a chamber for the night," said Rosalind. "When you invited me to stay with you, you could hardly have expected to put up my entire family."

"Oh, pooh!" Georgina answered, with a careless wave of her hand. Her ruby betrothal ring flashed in the firelight. "We must have a hundred guest chambers in this place, and no one to fill them. Mr. Lucas is welcome to stay as long as he likes."

Rosalind's lips tightened. "He will not stay long. Tomorrow, he will be going back to Cambridge, where he belongs."

Georgina laughed. "Rosie dear, I fear he will not be in any shape to travel tomorrow!"

Emily, who had been staring thoughtfully out of one of the windows, turned serious eyes to them. Rosalind wondered what she was thinking of; usually, Rosalind was adept at reading young ladies, but she found Lady Emily to be a mystery. Emily, in her third Season, was older than most of the misses on the Marriage Mart, and had seen far more of life than they had. She might look like a china shepherdess, with her golden curls and china blue eyes, but she was shrewd and did not miss much around her.

Her words showed that. "I am of the mind that Mr. Lucas could never have conceived of such a prank alone. He is too good-hearted, and was far too foxed."

"Do you suppose it was that silly Mr. Gilmore?" Georgina asked. "Or perhaps Lord Carteret. I saw them both there, in their costumes. They must have had a part in it."

Rosalind sat up with interest. She remembered Allen saying the original gaming debt had been owed to someone named Carteret at his club. "I fear I know little of Allen's friends in Town. He does not care to confide in his *sister* about them. What are these young men like?"

"Oh, they fancy themselves quite the rogues,"

Georgina said. "But really they are just mutton-heads, causing nuisances. They are often racketing about Town in the phaetons their fathers bought them, racing and throwing things."

"They belong to the same club as Mr. Lucas," Emily said. "The Thoth Club."

Oh, yes. Rosalind *had* heard of that club. The blasted club where Allen went to run up debts he could ill afford. "Is it a popular club?"

"Quite," Georgina said. "And now becoming harder to gain a membership, since so many have joined. Some would say your brother is very fortunate to be a member."

Rosalind gave an inelegant snort.

Georgina and Emily laughed and Lady Kate barked. "I quite agree," said Georgina. "Men and their clubs! I have sometimes thought of starting one myself, a sensible one for women only."

"Or one for artists?" Emily suggested. "But I do believe they have artists in the Thoth Club."

"Allen is not an artist," commented Rosalind. She would be glad if he *did* show an interest in art, or in anything besides carelessness.

"One can be of any sort of artistic bent at the Thoth Club—painting, music, literature, or even just possess an appreciation of such things," Emily said. "It was begun by Viscount Morley and Sir William Beene, another Society poet."

Of course. Rosalind remembered the particulars about that club now. She also remembered, with a hot flash of shame, how close she had been to Lord Morley in that dark corridor. If he had made another movement toward her, if Georgina had not appeared when she had . . .

Rosalind shivered to think what might have happened. Why, she might even have let the rogue *kiss* her!

She closed her eyes tightly to try to block out the memories, the images. When she opened them, she found Georgina watching her speculatively.

"Morley is quite handsome," Georgina commented. "Quite popular with the ladies."

"Oh, yes!" said Emily. "Did you see the way Lady Clarke was throwing herself at him tonight? Very scandalous. And that sort of thing happens everywhere he goes."

"I did not notice," Rosalind said, trying to sound careless and bored. To *feel* careless and bored. She certainly did not want to beg Emily to tell her more.

"How could you not notice, Rosie?" asked Georgina. "He certainly seemed to notice *you*."

Emily stared at Rosalind with avid wonder. "Did he, Mrs. Chase? What did he say to you? What did he *do*?"

"He did nothing, Lady Emily," Rosalind said tightly. "Your sister-in-law exaggerates. But it does not matter, for I fail to see Lord Morley's fabled charms." *Liar!* her mind screamed at her. "He may be handsome, but he has no manners. No man can be truly attractive without those."

Emily laughed. "Who cares about manners when a gentleman has such a handsome . . ."

"Emily!" Georgina cried, laughing. "You are meant to be an innocent young miss. Such a scandal you are."

Emily just shrugged. "I may be young, but I am not blind."

Even Rosalind had to laugh. "Right you are, Lady Emily. And such a handsome, mannerless man could have no interest in a woman such as me."

"You underestimate yourself, Rosie," Georgina argued. "You always did, even when we were in school."

"Indeed you do, Mrs. Chase," agreed Emily. "You had so many admirers tonight. I can't count the number of people who asked me about you."

"Only because they were trying to ingratiate themselves with *you,* Lady Emily," Rosalind said.

"Emily is quite the belle of the Season," Georgina said. "And she was last Season, and the Season before that, as well!"

Emily laughed, and pushed herself up out of her chair. "That is now my cue to retire, before Georgie starts hinting that it is about time I accepted one of my suitors."

"I did not do any such thing!" Georgina protested.

"Oh, of course not. Not *you*, never," answered Emily, still laughing. "Good night, Georgie. Good night, Mrs. Chase. Be careful, or she will start matchmaking for you, too."

"Good night, Lady Emily," said Rosalind. "Don't worry—I would never let her."

When the door had closed behind Emily, Georgina fell back onto her settee with a sigh, Lady Kate clambering up onto her lap. "I do sometimes worry about her, Rosie."

"Worry? About Lady Emily? She seems quite well to me."

"Oh, yes, she is. But this is her third Season. She has turned down at least two dozen offers." Georgina sighed. "I fear she will never find a man to love as I love my Alex. As you loved your Charles."

Charles. Yes, once Rosalind *had* thought she loved him. Not in the same way Georgina loved her duke, but with a quiet affection. He had been so well-mannered, so thoughtful. Now, sometimes, she had a difficult time recalling his face. Or the sound of his voice.

She shook her head sadly. This was no time to be maudlin! She was just tired—tired, and worried.

"Oh, Georgie," she said, with a weak little chuckle. "I would much rather worry about marrying off a duke's beautiful sister than try to convince my cabbage-head of a brother to behave sensibly."

Georgina leaned forward to squeeze Rosalind's hand reassuringly. "It is true that Mr. Lucas behaved badly tonight. But he is young! We were all young and foolish at one time. After a day or two, no one will speak of this incident at all. Something new and more scandalous will take its place."

"Yes, I know. But then he will do something else,

and then something *else,* and then . . ." And then—
they would be ruined. No one would trust their daughters to her care; her publisher would not buy any
more books.

It was all suddenly too much. Too much to bear
alone. Her exhaustion, her strange, unruly feelings for
Lord Morley, her brother's bad behavior—it was overwhelming. She covered her face with her hands, and
choked back a sob. But it would not be choked back;
it broke free, followed by another and another.

"Rosie!" Georgina cried. She put aside Lady Kate
and knelt down beside Rosalind in a rustle of silk.
"Oh, my dear, what is it? It must be more than what
happened tonight. I have never seen you so set-to.
Tell me what is wrong, please. Let me help you, if
I can."

Her friend's kindness was simply too much for Rosalind. Everything poured out of her—the book, the
school, the loans and debts Allen had accrued. Everything—everything, that is, except for Lord Morley. She
could not bring herself to tell even Georgina about
that. Whatever it was.

When it had all drained from her in a torrent of
tears and incoherent words, Rosalind fell back, de-
pleted, into her chair. She slumped down, forgetting
even the rules of proper posture.

Georgina stared up at her with wide, shocked green
eyes. Rosalind thought vaguely that this must be a
moment to remember. She had never seen Georgina
shocked before.

"*You* wrote *A Lady's Rules*?" Georgina whispered.
"You, Rosie? And you never told me?"

"I have told no one," Rosalind answered. "I must
be discreet, for the sake of my school, and I feared
that even something so harmless as an etiquette book
could bring unwanted attention."

"But you are famous!" cried Georgina. "Or at least
A Lady is. Everyone adores your book."

"Or they did—until recently. My publisher says that

sales are falling, and they do not want to publish a planned second edition."

Georgina sat back on her heels. "So that is why you came to London. To investigate."

"I did hope perhaps I could discover something that might be of use," Rosalind admitted.

"And you found it is Lord Morley who is breaking your rules!" Georgina's eyes sparkled, and her lips curved in a grin. "And that is why you were with him in the corridor. To make him confess."

Rosalind could see she just had to nip this in the bud. Georgina was much too fond of intrigues, schemes, and romances. She read too many horrid novels. She was quite capable of making all of this into some grand drama. "Now, Georgina, listen . . ." she began.

"Here you are, ladies!" the duke's voice interrupted. Rosalind turned to see Georgina's husband standing in the doorway, a tray with a bottle of fine brandy and some glasses in his hand. "I thought after such a strange evening a brandy might be in order."

"Alex, my darling, you are an angel," Georgina said. She sat back in her chair, but tossed Rosalind a glance that promised this discussion was not finished. "You have read my mind yet again."

Rosalind usually did not imbibe brandy. But tonight, it sounded exactly what she needed. "Thank you, Your Grace," she murmured, and accepted the glass of lovely amber liquid.

"Now, Mrs. Chase, I have asked you many times to call me Alexander," he said, and sat down on the arm of his wife's chair.

"Of course—Alexander," Rosalind said, though it still did not feel quite right to call a duke by his given name!

"Very good," said Alexander. "And you will be happy to know that your brother is safely asleep in the Green Room. No worse for wear, though he will have a demon of a headache in the morning."

Rosalind gave him a grateful smile, and sipped at her brandy. For now, for this one moment, it felt so very good to let someone else help her, to let at least a tiny portion of the burden drop away.

She would have to pick it up again soon enough.

Allen was already tucked up in bed when Rosalind looked in on him as she made her way to her own chamber. He looked exhausted and wan against the clean white linens, but he sat up smartly enough when she entered the room, pulling the blankets up to his chin.

"Rosie!" he cried. "For heaven's sake, I have retired. You shouldn't be in here!"

Ordinarily, Rosalind would agree. It was against the rules for a lady to enter a man's chamber, even that of her brother. Tonight, though, after everything that had happened, such niceties seemed faintly ridiculous. She had to talk to Allen, and she had to do it now.

She waved away his sputtering protests and sat down on a chair by the bed. "Allen, please do not be missish. I watched the nursemaid change your nappies when you were two months old; it scarcely matters if I see you in your nightshirt now."

"Oh, Rosie," Allen muttered miserably, sinking down against the pillows.

"I wanted to talk to you now," Rosalind went on, "but I promise I will be quick. I am very tired, as no doubt you are. It was a most *turbulent* evening."

Allen looked even more miserable, if that was possible. "I never meant for you to find out about that. If I had known you were there . . ."

"I know you are sorry now, Allen. And I am sorry, too."

Allen's bloodshot eyes widened in surprise. "*You,* Rosie? What are you sorry for?"

"I have only just now realized something, and that is that I still think of you as that baby in nappies, and not as the young man that you are. I was so much older than you, eleven years old when you were born, that I have always felt I had to look after you. Now I see that I need to help you look after yourself."

"What do you mean?" Allen appeared profoundly confused, and really, Rosalind thought, who could blame him? He had never had to take care of himself before, as Rosalind had always swooped in to do it for him. But she was tired now, so very tired. She could be his caretaker no longer.

"I mean that I have done you a disservice. I have lectured you about your careless behavior, and exhorted you to cease your gaming. But I have not told you of our true situation, which would have helped you to see the right path for yourself."

Rosalind closed her eyes, took a deep breath—and told her brother the truth of their financial situation. She told him about *A Lady's Rules,* the expenses of the school, the letters from the bank. She told all this in the shortest, sparest language she could find, but when she was done she still felt drained. She slumped back in her chair and opened her eyes.

Allen had left the bed in silence and knelt on the carpet beside her chair. He looked so very young, with his overlarge borrowed nightshirt and tousled hair. But his eyes—his eyes glowed with a faint light that was years older.

"So you see, Allen, that there is enough money for your education," she told him. "Indeed, I am happy to give you that. But there is not enough for any more debts. It cannot go on, or we will be ruined. That is as plainly as I can say it."

Allen shook his head, his jaw working as if he *wanted* to say something but could not find the words. Then he said, "I am sorry, Rosie. So sorry. I should have realized—should have known. You always said . . ."

"I tried to protect you, as our parents wished."

"You do not need to *protect* me! I am a grown man now. I should be protecting *you.*"

"All I want is for you to return to school, to prepare for a career. That is all I ever wished for."

He clasped her hand between his. "I will, Rosie. I will go back tomorrow, and will make up things with my tutor. I swear it."

Rosalind smiled at him wearily. "Thank you, Allen dear. That is all I could ask for."

Chapter Twelve

"Never make a glutton of yourself in public. Sip daintily at tea, and only take small nibbles of the lightest of foods."
-A Lady's Rules for Proper Behavior, Chapter Eight

*M*ichael drew his phaeton to a halt outside the Waylands's townhouse, and stared up at its white marble façade. In its way, it was even more grand than Bronston House, with its classical pediments and multiple chimneys and sparkling windows. By all rights, it should be twice as forbidding, since it housed a ducal household. But the bright green draperies at the first floor windows, the potted topiaries that lined the front walk, and the redheaded moppet of a child who peered down from one of the upper story windows, gave it a life, a welcoming air, that Bronston House could never hope to possess.

He feared that one of the residents of the house would not be nearly so welcoming, though. In fact, he would be quite fortunate if Mrs. Chase did not toss him down those front steps on his backside. He was not her favorite person in the world—he knew that from the cold stare she had given him in the Portmans' ballroom last night, but that did not change his own feelings. He wanted to see her; he *had* to see her, no matter in what state he found her this morning, even if she shouted at him and *did* throw him out.

The image of the dainty, proper Mrs. Chase pushing

him onto the pavement like some avenging etiquette goddess made him smile. That smile faded when the front door opened and a black-coated butler appeared. Michael would *have* to go in now that he had been spotted.

He handed the reins to a footman who appeared beside the phaeton, and jumped down to the walkway to enter the house.

"Good morning, sir," the butler said, holding out a small silver card tray.

"Good morning," Michael answered. He dug out a card from inside his coat and deposited it properly upon the tray. Even Mrs. Chase would have to approve. "I am calling to see if the duchess and Mrs. Chase are at home."

"I will endeavor to ascertain that, Lord Morley." The butler bowed, and retreated into a room off the foyer, shutting the door behind him.

Michael was only alone in the marble and satin silence for a moment. He had tilted his head to examine a painting on the wall, a sweeping Italian landscape bearing the duchess's own signature, when a voice said from behind him, "Who are *you*?"

He turned to see the redheaded moppet he had glimpsed in the window. Now she stood on the grand staircase, peering down at him from over the carved balustrade. She could not be more than about four, a tiny doll with long curls and freckles. She picked up the trailing streamers of her pink satin sash and popped them into her mouth.

Michael grinned, and gave her his lowest, most elegant bow. "I am Viscount Morley. And to whom do I have the great honor of speaking? A fairy princess, surely."

The little sprite giggled. "I am Lady Elizabeth Anne."

"How do you do, my lady."

She took a step down. "I have a brother. His name is Sebastian, but he's only tiny and can't talk. Mama says it will be a long time before he can play with me."

"I am sorry to hear that."

"He is utterly useless." She gave a deep sigh.

Michael laughed. Surely it was the story of brothers everywhere, to be found useless by their sisters. He had the feeling that Violet would agree with Lady Elizabeth Anne. "I am certain he will prove more, er, useful when he is a bit older. Infants do grow quite quickly, you know."

She shook her head, her curls bouncing. "No. It will not be soon enough." She took another step, and gave him a speculative glance that quite belied her tender years. She was the very image of the duchess. "You look as if *you* could be useful. I need someone to tie a rope from that chandelier."

"Why?" he asked suspiciously.

"So I can swing from it, of course."

Michael tilted back his head to stare up—*far* up—at the Venetian glass chandelier that hung from the domed ceiling. *The little minx.* She had only known him for two minutes and she was already trying to break his neck. It was surely a harbinger of what he could expect from the ladies in this house.

Before he could answer her, the door the butler had disappeared behind opened. Michael turned, expecting to see the man there now.

Instead he saw Mrs. Chase herself. She stood in the doorway, one hand braced on the wooden frame. Gone was the sea green clad siren of the night before; gone was her wealth of red hair, the sheen of pearls against white skin. She again wore one of her caps, a hideous white muslin affair, and a morning gown of gray and black striped muslin. A plain white chemisette was tucked into her neckline, and covered her almost to the chin.

Michael almost groaned at the acute sense of loss that pierced him at the sight. For one moment, one sublime second, in Lady Portman's corridor, he had glimpsed the *real* Rosalind, a woman of great allure and an untapped fire that could burn as bright as her glorious hair.

At least, he had hoped, *desired* that that was the true Rosalind. But perhaps this woman before him now was truly her, the woman who stared at him with no expression at all on her face. Her gaze was cool.

"Lord Morley," she said, her voice equally expressionless. Her gaze slid past him, and a warm smile curved her lips, illuminating her pale face. "Elizabeth Anne, whatever are you doing here?" She swept past him and up the stairs to take the child by the hand.

"I wanted to see our visitor," Elizabeth Anne said, hugging close to Mrs. Chase's skirts. "He is going to tie a rope to the chandelier for me to swing from."

Mrs. Chase shot him a hard glare, as if she believed him capable of hurtling infants through the air. "I am sure he is *not,* dear. Now, why don't you go into the drawing room and see your mother and Aunt Emily. I will be there in just a moment."

"Is *he* going to stay, too?" Elizabeth Anne asked. "When there is a caller, cook sends up tea and almond cakes."

"We will see, dear. Now run along, and remember— no more nonsense about swinging from ropes."

Elizabeth Anne peeped up at Mrs. Chase. "Because it would be against *A Lady's Rules,* Aunt Rosalind?" Before Mrs. Chase could answer, the child hopped down the remaining steps and dashed across the foyer to disappear into the drawing room.

Michael stared after her, stunned. So now *babies* had to follow the rules? It was too much. Surely even swinging from a rope would be preferable.

But he could not think of that now, could not allow himself to become angry. He had come here to apologize. Arguing with Mrs. Chase about rules would not smooth his way at all.

She still stood there on the stairs, looking down at him. The glow that had animated her features when she spoke to the child had faded as if it had never been.

"We did not expect to see you today," she said, ever so politely. "If you would care to come into the drawing room, I am sure the duchess would be happy to receive you."

"I actually came to see *you*, Mrs. Chase," he said.

Her eyes widened. "To see *me*?"

"Yes. I wanted to apologize."

"Apologize? For encouraging my brother to make some sort of drunken raid on the Portman ball?" Her eyes were not ice now—they burned with a deep blue fire. She stepped gracefully down to the foot of the staircase, her fingers clenched on the stone balustrade. "For urging him once again to behave in a most irresponsible manner?"

Michael could feel the entire situation slipping out of his control. Of course he had wanted to inquire after Lucas after his little "adventure" last night, but really it had not been such a great thing. When Michael left the ball, Lucas's escapade had been all but forgotten. And he had certainly never *encouraged* such a thing!

"I fear I had no prior knowledge of your brother's plans at all, Mrs. Chase," he said tightly. "You can be assured that if I had, I would have done everything in my power to discourage him."

Her frown spoke volumes of doubt. "Then what *did* you come to apologize for, Lord Morley?"

"I came to apologize for—monopolizing your time at the ball last night." That seemed the most polite way to say *for cornering you in the dark*. "And to return this."

He drew her folded fan from inside his coat and held it out to her.

"My fan," she whispered. She moved closer to him, and took the scrap of satin and lace from his hand, careful not to let her fingers brush his. She spread it wide, staring down at its glistening expanse. It seemed some sort of artifact from the lost beauty of the night before, held so gently by the woman who had buried that beauty beneath layers of gray muslin.

But he could see now that she was not entirely submerged. She stood so close to him he could see the shadow of pale golden freckles under a dusting of rice powder, could smell the fresh green springtime scent of her perfume. As he watched, a faint pink flush spread across her cheekbones.

It was as if she, too, remembered their moments alone last night. Maybe she also felt the unmistakable draw between them now, his temptation to take off that absurd cap and let her hair spill down . . .

She darted a quick, startled glance at him from beneath her lashes. "Thank you for returning this," she said. Her voice was still tinged with coolness, but he fancied marginally less so than it had been when she first saw him here. Or perhaps that was just his own wishful thinking. "Would you care to come into the drawing room?"

"Yes," he answered. "I do so enjoy—almond cakes."

Her blush deepened to a rose tinge, and she brushed past him to hurry back to the drawing room.

Oh, yes, Michael thought. He was assuredly making progress with her.

She was *not* glad to see him. She was merely being polite. It would never do to quarrel with the wicked man in her friend's home.

That is what Rosalind told herself, anyway, as she led Lord Morley into the drawing room. She tried to forget the tiny, excited skipping beat of her heart when she saw him standing there in the foyer. It was probably only dismay that he had dared to appear so soon after the disaster of the Portman ball. Or it was the marmalade from her breakfast tray disagreeing with her.

Yes! she thought, seizing on that excuse. Her queasiness, her nervousness, had nothing to do with this man at all. It was marmalade.

Even if he did appear rather handsome this morning, the dark waves of his hair in disarray from the wind, his face bronzed from the sun . . .

No! Rosalind curled her hands tightly into fists and

pressed them against her skirt. It was merely that marmalade, disagreeing with her again. All would be well once she had a sensible meal.

Or once Lord Morley took himself off and left them in peace.

The scene in the drawing room was peacefully domestic, and its very ordinariness helped Rosalind to catch her breath. Georgina and Emily were seated next to the small fire that burned in the grate against the morning chill. Emily worked on a piece of embroidery, while Georgina was bent over her sketchbook. On a footstool by her mother's side, Elizabeth Anne wielded a stick of charcoal over her own tiny sketchbook, all thoughts of swinging from the chandelier apparently forgotten for the moment. Lady Kate slept in her velvet dog bed.

Georgina looked up, and gave their guest one of her charming smiles. "Lord Morley! What a pleasant surprise to see you here this morning."

Rosalind seated herself on one of the brocade settees, watching as Michael bowed to Georgina and said, "I trust I have not called at an inconvenient time. I wanted to see how Mr. Lucas fared."

"Of course it is not an inconvenient time! You have saved us from a very dull morning. And I believe Mr. Lucas is quite well. He just rang for some wash water and coffee, so I am certain we will see him down here soon. Would you not say so, Rosalind?"

Rosalind, who was trying to concentrate on little Elizabeth Anne and *not* on staring at Lord Morley, glanced at Georgina in surprise. "What? Oh, yes. Indeed."

"So you see," Georgina said to Morley, "no harm done at all. I see you also found Mrs. Chase's fan."

Rosalind stared down dumbly at the fan she still held, clutched in her fist. She had forgotten it was there. "Yes, Lord Morley very kindly returned it to me. I must have—have misplaced it last night."

"I thought you might be in need of it, Mrs. Chase," Lord Morley said quietly.

Rosalind glanced up to find him watching her, his expression uncharacteristically serious. There was no hint of his usual teasing grin, the laughing gleam in his eye. "Thank you," she murmured.

Georgina smiled radiantly, as if a great dark cloud of tension did not hover over her elegant drawing room. "Won't you please be seated, Lord Morley? Elizabeth Anne, dearest, why don't you ring for some tea?"

Elizabeth Anne leaped to her feet in a flurry of ribbons and curls. "And almond cakes, too, Mama? Please?"

Georgina laughed. "Very well, my darling, almond cakes, too. Though Nanny will be furious with me for letting you have sweets in the middle of the morning."

Lord Morley sat down on a chair uncomfortably close to Rosalind's settee. She resisted the urge to pull her skirts closer, to tuck herself away for some measure of safety. She so hated it that whenever he came near, whenever he was even in the same room, she became someone who was—was not herself. Not sensible Rosalind, who had taken care of herself and her family with no assistance for so many years, who was always calm, always competent. Always the one her friends and pupils looked to to provide an example of propriety.

When she was near him, as she was now, she became someone she could not know and did not like. Someone who felt foolish and fluttery, and very young. Which was silly in the extreme, since she was lately turned thirty, and he was probably younger than her by some years. A young man who wrote romantic poetry about love and passion and the physical world, who brazenly flirted with women in ballrooms and school drawing rooms.

Rosalind resolutely put the satin fan down on a nearby table and folded her hands in her lap. She was very glad that she wore one of her own serviceable garments, and not one of the colorful frocks Georgina was always pressing on her with the excuse that she had ordered them from the mantua-maker and now did not like them. Even if Rosalind did not *feel* like herself, she could *look* like herself, and perhaps that would be enough to fool the people around her.

If only Lord Morley would not stare at her so intently! It was as if—as if he tried to look past the yards of plain gray muslin and see into her very heart.

Rosalind thanked heaven for Georgina, who kept up a steady stream of polite chatter, and for Elizabeth Anne, who insisted on serving the tea herself and caused a great distraction by spilling it on the inlaid chinoiserie tea table.

Once the refreshments had been safely distributed, Elizabeth Anne came to sit by Rosalind, and leaned against her side. Rosalind put her arm about her, and breathed in her sweet, powdery, little-girl smell. It was comforting, real, and it reminded her of all she had to protect—her school, where girls just like this would be waiting for her when the holiday was finished.

"I'm going to go to Aunt Rosalind's school," Elizabeth Anne told Lord Morley. "That's where I am going to learn to be a grand lady. Mama says Aunt Rosalind is the best at turning little hoydens like me into grand ladies, though really I would rather be a bareback rider at Astley's."

"I will be most honored to have a future bareback rider at the Seminary," Rosalind said with a laugh. "Though you are too young right now, Elizabeth Anne. Perhaps in a year or two."

"I am sure you will enjoy it at Mrs. Chase's school, Lady Elizabeth Anne," Lord Morley said. "My sister is a pupil there, and she speaks very highly of your— Aunt Rosalind."

"You have a sister?" Elizabeth Anne looked at him with wide, wondering green eyes, as if she could not imagine he could possibly possess something so ordinary as a sister. Rosalind sometimes wondered at that herself. "Is she like me?"

"She is as pretty as you," he said. "But she is several years older. She will soon be graduating from the Seminary, and making her bow next Season."

"How is Lady Violet?" Rosalind asked, watching Elizabeth Anne as she took another cake. "I have been hoping to see her while I am in Town, but I am sure she has been quite busy."

"We have been to the theater, and to a few suppers at our aunt's home, but she has not been as busy as she would like. I am sure she would enjoy it very much if you were to call on her. In fact . . ." He broke off, and gave her an uncertain glance.

"Yes, Lord Morley?" she asked.

"I was just going to say that I am taking Violet to Gunter's this afternoon for ices. Perhaps you would care to join us, Mrs. Chase? And the duchess and Lady Emily, of course." He sounded oddly shy as he offered the invitation.

Rosalind saw Georgina and Emily exchange a significant glance between them, and she felt her cheeks heat again. In these last two days, she had blushed more than she had in the last ten years! And right now it was all due to those two incorrigible matchmakers. They spent hours gossiping and scheming about all their friends. They probably imagined there was something untoward between herself and Lord Morley. It would have been angering if it was not so laughable.

"Oh, Emily and I have an appointment at the—at the milliner," Georgina said. "But I am sure Rosalind would welcome the chance to escape such a dull outing."

"May I go, too, Mama?" Elizabeth Anne begged. "I love Gunter's!"

"No, darling," Georgina answered. "It is a grown-up outing."

Rosalind studied Lord Morley closely, trying to gauge the sincerity of his invitation. Did he truly wish her to come along? Or was he just being polite?

And what did *she* truly wish to do? She wanted to

see Violet again, to be certain the girl was faring well in Town. And the thought of an entire afternoon looking at bonnets she could not afford to buy was not appealing, though she was almost certain Georgina had just made that up as an excuse. After all, who made an appointment to see a milliner? Ices at Gunter's with Violet sounded much finer.

But the thought of an entire afternoon with Lord Morley was—unsettling, even if he proved to be sincere in his invitation.

Rosalind prided herself on being a generous lady. Surely Lord Morley deserved a chance to atone for his bad behavior, and she deserved the chance to ask him to leave Allen alone. To try to fulfill her mission in London, which was to restore the rules and the proper order of things.

Yes, she decided, she *would* allow him to make amends. With a strawberry ice.

"Very well, Lord Morley," she said. "I would be happy to join you and Lady Violet at Gunter's this afternoon."

He smiled, a wide, white grin that dazzled as the sun breaking forth on a dreary winter's day. "Excellent! I am sure Violet will be in alt when I tell her. Would two o'clock suit?"

"Yes, thank you," Rosalind answered politely. "That would suit very well."

She had surely just completely lost her mind. The moment the acceptance passed her lips, she had the wild desire to pull it back, to stay safely alone in the house for the rest of the day.

It was too late, though. Georgina and Emily were chattering again, asking Lord Morley about his newest volume of poems. Elizabeth Anne was pirouetting around the furniture. And, as if it was all not cacophonous enough, the door opened and Allen appeared.

He was paler than usual, but otherwise did not appear to be damaged in any way by his escapade at the Portman ball. He was even rather better groomed than usual, with clean boots, unwrinkled trousers, and a crisply tied cravat. If only he did not look quite so morose.

"Morley!" he cried happily, his strained, white face transformed from melancholy to avid interest in an instant. "By Jove, but it's good to see you again. Didn't know you were expected." He stepped forward to shake hands with Lord Morley, and added, in a quieter tone, "I'm afraid I made a bit of a cake of myself last night."

A bit of a cake? Rosalind almost choked. Her brother had made a veritable pastry kitchen out of himself. She held her tongue, though. It would not serve her cause if she embarrassed Allen in front of his hero Lord Morley. It would not serve her cause at all.

She would just have to bide her time—until this afternoon.

Chapter Thirteen

"Always be gracious when introduced to new acquaintances."
~~A~~ *Lady's Rules for Proper Behavior,*   Chapter Eleven

"*D*o you really mean it, Michael? We are going to see Mrs. Chase today?" Violet practically bounced on her toes in her enthusiasm, her hands clasped under her chin. A delighted giggle bubbled from her lips.

Michael couldn't help but smile at her happiness. She *had* smiled a few times since they came to Town, and even laughed at the play they had attended. But he had not seen her eyes sparkle so in—well, in a very long time. And it was due to Mrs. Chase. Somber, straightlaced Mrs. Chase, who was not quite as prim and proper as she would like everyone, including herself, to believe.

Violet almost spun about in a joyous circle, but then, with a visible effort, brought her exuberance under control. She folded her hands in front of her, and recited, " 'A lady never displays her joy in an unseemly, physical manner.' " Then she gave a tiny jump and another smile. "*Do* you mean it, Michael? Mrs. Chase is in London and we are to see her?"

"Of course I mean it, Vi," Michael said, with a laugh to cover his irritation at her rule-spouting. "She is going to Gunter's with us. I met her at a ball last night, and she asked after you." He decided to omit the quite unnecessary details of everything that had happened after his initial encounter with her at the Portman ball.

"A *ball*," Violet sighed. "It must have been lovely." Her smile turned wistful.

Michael put his arm about her shoulders and gave her a comforting squeeze. She did not draw away, as she had so often of late when minding the rules. "Next Season, you will attend more balls than you could count," he said. "So many you will be longing for a quiet evening at home!"

Violet laughed, a strangely bitter sound, unlike her earlier happy giggles. "I cannot imagine ever longing for *that*."

Michael frowned. "Has Father been bullying you?"

"No, of course not." She pulled away from him and went to look into a mirror hanging on the morning room wall. She fluffed up her pale curls, not meeting his reflected gaze. "I have been trying to educate him on some of the rules. Just because he never leaves the house is no excuse for him not to be civilized. He took exception to one of them this morning and threw his stick at me."

"He did *what*?" Michael shouted. "Did that old barbarian hurt you?"

"Oh, no, no. I am quite adept at dodging. And I am certain there must be a rule against stick-throwing. I shall have to look it up." Violet reached for her bonnet and tied it over her hair, tucking stray curls up into its confinement. She was trying so hard to be calm and casual, but her movements were stiff.

Michael longed to storm into his father's room, grab that blasted stick out of the old man's gnarled hands, and break it over his head.

Violet obviously sensed his inner turmoil, for she reached out and laid her hand gently on his arm. "Oh, la, Michael, but you *have* turned all red! Please do not mind it. I hardly see him, really, for you and Aunt Minnie keep me so very busy. Soon enough I will be back at school. And this afternoon I will see Mrs.

Chase! Speaking of which, shall we be going? She will be expecting us."

She picked up her shawl and handed it to him for him to drape over her shoulders. Then she took his hand and guided him to the front door, obviously trying to hurry him out of the house.

Michael went along with her maneuverings. It would be too bad of him to start yet another quarrel in this house, when she so badly wanted this outing. But one day—one day soon—matters in this family would erupt.

Right now, though, they had this afternoon. And he was going to make very sure it was enjoyable for his sister, and for Mrs. Chase. Surely the woman just had to see that he was not the lout she thought him. An hour or two in Gunter's, with the warm, sugary smells of pastries around them and a luscious strawberry ice to savor, would be just the thing.

She was making a great mistake. She should stay home and work on her writing, or her embroidery, or *anything* rather than go out with Lord Morley.

But that would be cowardly, Rosalind told herself, and it certainly would not help her in her cause at all. She had to make Morley see the error of his rude ways, and she could never do that by hiding away in the house. She truly wanted to see Lady Violet, too, and be certain the girl was faring well.

She paced back to the window for the tenth time to peer down at the street. Lord Morley was not there yet, but many pedestrians and carriages crowded on the pavement outside Wayland House. She studied the passersby, fiddling idly with the braid trim at the wrist of her spencer. For just one instant, she wished she had borrowed one of Georgina's walking dresses, of vivid blue or wine red or tawny gold. Her sensible dark blue wool, with its pale yellow braid trim, was just so very—sensible. That was the only word for it.

Of course it is, she told herself sternly. *You are a sensible lady.*

She half-turned to pluck up the hat Georgina *had* convinced her to borrow, then peered down again at the street as she pinned it to her curls. It was the same swirl of humanity, but, as Rosalind's gaze moved over the crowd, it was somehow caught by the figure of a man across the street. He leaned idly against the fence that hemmed in a small park in the square, apparently just a careless man-about-town with nothing better to do than lounge about, observing passing females. There was nothing remarkable about him at all; he was of middling height, slim, well-dressed but not os-tentatious. The brim of his hat concealed his features.

Rosalind would not even have noticed him, except that he had been there for rather a long time—ever since she herself had come down and begun her vigil at the window. And he was oddly intent. He gave the appearance of watching the other people, yet he never really turned his attention from Wayland House.

Rosalind frowned. She was strangely reminded of that evening at her school, when she had been looking out the window of her sitting room and thought, or imagined, she saw a movement in the garden.

"Don't be silly," she whispered aloud. "You are becoming delusional."

Perhaps what she needed was a seaside holiday, away from all the distractions of Town. Away from Lord Morley.

She gazed down again at the man. If he was there again tomorrow, she would tell Georgina or the duke. Today, though, she would just enjoy her time with Lady Violet.

As she watched, a carriage drew to a halt below her window. It was a proper open landau, driven by a coachman in livery, not Morley's usual dashing pha-eton. But she would have recognized the figure who leaped jauntily to the pavement, even if he had arrived in a stuffy old barouche. His head was uncovered, his dark hair tossed about, a glossy blue-black in the sun-light. His coat fell back as he turned to offer his hand to his sister, revealing a waistcoat embroidered with red flowers and a cravat of deep yellow.

"Good heavens, Rosalind!" she said to herself. "Imagine that. You are about to go out in public with a man who wears *yellow* cravats. And forgets his hat."

That ought to fill her with horror, ought to make her run into her chamber and lock the door. But instead it gave her a tiny, tingling thrill that had nothing to do with *horror* at all.

Rosalind pushed all these thoughts away, and turned to make her way down the stairs just as the butler opened the door to admit Lord Morley and Lady Violet. Rosalind paused to be sure her hair was still pinned neatly beneath the hat, then went down to greet them properly.

"Lady Violet, Lord Morley," she said. "How delightful to see you."

"Mrs. Chase!" Violet cried, and rushed over to take Rosalind's hand. The girl was obviously trying to behave with the utmost propriety, but her eyes sparkled, and her gloved fingers curled tightly over Rosalind's own. It was quite a relief to see the girl looking so well. "I could scarcely believe it when Michael told me you were *here,* in London. I thought I would not see you again until I returned to the Seminary."

"The school is far too quiet with all of you girls gone," Rosalind said. "I am very happy to see you, too, Lady Violet. You seem very well indeed."

"My brother has been keeping me busy, taking me to the theater and such," Violet replied. "It has been very merry! This will be the third time we have been to Gunter's. I am quite in alt over their strawberry ices!"

"Well, I have never been there before, so I shall rely on your guidance in making my choices," Rosalind told her.

"You have never been to Gunter's!" Violet cried in evident horror. "Then we must go there now, at once. You will adore it, I vow! Won't she, Michael?"

Rosalind reluctantly turned her attention from Violet to the girl's brother. Lord Morley gave her a wide grin, and said, "Oh, yes, we should hurry. Some pleasures, Mrs. Chase, should never be delayed."

Before Rosalind could respond, Violet took her arm and drew her to the front door, with Lord Morley following behind. She was so caught up by the feel of his gloved hand on hers as he helped her into the carriage that she quite forgot to see if the lurking man was still there.

Gunter's was crowded with well-dressed members of the *ton,* gorging themselves on pastries and ices and glancing about avidly to see who else was there. It was exactly as if the Portman ballroom where Rosalind had first encountered Lord Morley in London had been moved in toto to the café. All the same people were there; the same snatches of conversation floated through the sugar-scented air. Only the jeweled hair combs and feathered turbans had been replaced by bonnets here.

As Lord Morley opened the door to usher Rosalind and Violet inside, Rosalind reached up to be sure her own hat was straight. It was one of Georgina's pieces of millinery, a tall-crowned, fashion-forward affair made of dark blue velvet and satin, with a flirtatious half veil of blue tulle. Rosalind had not been too sure of it when Georgina pressed it on her; unlike a proper bonnet or a cap, it left too much of her red hair exposed. But she had given in and worn the thing.

Now she wished more than ever for one of her own bonnets, preferably one with a concealing brim. When Michael stepped into the shop and offered an arm each to Rosalind and his sister, everyone turned to stare. A small hush fell over the café, but it was quickly dissipated, like a puff of smoke. Conversation resumed—yet people still watched. Rosalind saw Lady Clarke, who gave a tiny finger wave to Morley before leaning forward to whisper to her friends.

Rosalind stiffened her spine until she stood at her

full, not inconsiderable height, and tilted up her chin. She absolutely refused to let *anyone,* much less Lady Clarke, make her feel as if she did not belong here, on the arm of Lord Morley.

Morley himself seemed oblivious to the attention. No doubt he was accustomed to it, since it appeared to follow him wherever he went. Lady Violet, too, paid no heed, since she was too busy staring around with wide, amazed eyes.

"I believe I see a table over there by the wall," Lord Morley said. "Shall we?"

Rosalind glanced over at the table indicated. It was just big enough for three, in a relatively quiet corner. "It seems fine," Rosalind answered. "But do you not want to sit with one of your friends?"

A tiny, puzzled crease appeared between his velvety dark eyes. "My friends, Mrs. Chase?"

"Yes. Obviously many people here know you. I just saw Lady Clarke wave at you."

He laughed, a rich, merry sound that caused yet another wave of attention to crest in their direction. "No, Mrs. Chase. This afternoon I want only to be with my sister—and with you." His gaze lingered on hers, almost like a—a caress.

Rosalind felt her cheeks smolder again. Fortunately, Violet tugged at his arm then. "Michael," she said excitedly. "May I have one of those strawberry ices now?"

Lord Morley laughed again, and led them to the vacant table. "Vi, you may have as many ices as you like, and cakes, too."

"Truly?" Violet sighed, an utterly rapturous sound, and turned her attention to the small menu set before her.

"Anything you like." Michael turned to smile again at Rosalind. She couldn't help but think that he was well-named—Michael, the archangel. "And what would you care for, Mrs. Chase?"

What would she care for? Rosalind could scarcely consider cakes and pastries when he looked at her.

Indeed, she could scarcely think at all. She aimed her full attention on her gloves, tugging them slowly off her hands. She folded the pale blue kid and laid them atop the table.

"I think I shall just have some tea," she answered. She never removed her stare from the gloves.

"Just tea? Oh, no, no, Mrs. Chase," Morley chided teasingly. He reached out and touched her gloves, running one long, dark finger over the leather before laying his hand flat atop them. "You are at Gunter's. They are renowned for their decadent pastries. You cannot go back to the country without at least trying one."

Rosalind slowly raised her gaze to his. Much to her surprise, he was not smiling now. He was intent as he watched her, questioning—pleading? "Must I?" she murmured. The rich cakes seemed so very—decadent.

"I insist." His voice was husky.

"Oh, yes, Mrs. Chase! You cannot come to Gunter's and simply have a cup of tea. Try some marzipan," Violet piped up. Her young voice burst whatever spell of enchantment Rosalind had fallen under, and she was able to turn away from him at last.

She still felt him watching her, though, and even as he laughed with Violet she heard the darkness, the pull of him.

She needed something cold to drink. Cold, and very strong.

Michael watched as Mrs. Chase turned away from him, turned all her attention to Violet's prattlings. She even reached out and gently slid her gloves from beneath his hand and off the table, careful not to touch his skin.

He *felt* her, though, felt the warmth of her hand, the softness of her skin. She had the fairness of a redhead, with a few pale golden freckles sprinkled over the translucent back of her hand.

In his mind, he saw himself catch up that hand, pressing kisses to each of those tiny freckles, to the

faint blue of the veins in her slim wrist, her delicate
fingers. He could almost feel her pulse throbbing beneath his lips . . .

Michael sat back in his chair, sucking in a deep
breath of the sweet air. Even then he could not entirely escape those strange feelings, for he could smell
her fresh, green-spring perfume.

He could not escape them whenever he was in her
presence, for these sensations drew him in, drowned
him, just as they had in her office, in the dark corridor
at the Portman ball. There was just something about
Mrs. Chase, something mysterious and alluring and
deep. He wanted to discover what that was—he
needed to know.

But he could not discover anything here. He would
have to find a way to see her again, someplace more
quiet. Yet how to persuade her to see him? She was
as skittish as a new colt; she did not even want him
touching her gloves. He would just have to find a way,
that was all.

"Morley!" someone called out.

Michael looked back to see Sir William Beene, a
fellow poet who had helped to found the Thoth Club.
Will was one of his best cronies; they had spent many
hours discussing literature, music, and the damnable
fickleness of the muse.

Michael stood up to shake hands with Will—and
then saw his friend's gaze land on Mrs. Chase and
kindle with avid interest.

"Morley, old man," Will purred. "Won't you introduce me to this lovely lady? It would be a great sin
for you to keep her to yourself."

And, even as he made the introductions and
watched Mrs. Chase smile at Will, he had the strongest
urge to plant his good friend a facer.

It was rather late when Michael returned to his own
lodgings. He had gone for a drive in the park with
Violet and Mrs. Chase after Gunter's, had stayed with
his sister until she went off to the theater with Aunt

Minnie. So the steps leading to his rooms were dimly lit in the gloaming, and he did not see the figure seated on the top step until he very nearly tripped over him. Michael nearly went sprawling, his foot landing on soft flesh.

"What the devil . . ." He automatically lifted his walking stick to defend himself, though the light, carved wood would actually be less than useless in a brawl.

"Oh, no, Morley, don't hit me! It's Allen Lucas."

"Lucas?" Michael slowly lowered the stick, and peered through the gloom to see that it was indeed Mrs. Chase's brother. "Why are you skulking about here outside my rooms?"

"I was just waiting for you," Lucas said, scrambling to his feet. His coat and cravat were rumpled, as if he had been wearing them for too long, but he looked much better than he had after his escapade at the Portman ball. His eyes were clear, his face not so pale. He seemed as if he had grown up in only a few days. "I am going back to Cambridge, but I wanted to talk with you before I left."

"Why couldn't you just leave a card? There was no need for you to take up residence on the staircase." Michael pushed his door open, and ushered the young man into his rooms. The draperies were drawn back at the windows, letting in the last dying rays of sunlight, and he went about lighting the lamps.

Lucas sat down in one of the armchairs by the fireplace, twisting his hat in his hands. When Michael finished his task, he sat down across from Lucas, and waited for the young man to state his errand.

"I wanted to talk to you about m'sister," Lucas said, in a great rush as if to corral his courage, though Michael could not imagine why it took courage to speak of *her*. "She is not at all happy with me, you see."

"Well, your behavior at the Portman ball *was* rather foolish. I imagine she was quite embarrassed."

Lucas shook his head. "No, it is more than that. I have not seen our true circumstances, though heaven knows she has tried to tell me enough times. She has always been more like a mother to me than a sister, you see. Our parents died when I was very young, and she's always worked so hard to take care of me. I never realized *how* hard until recently. I got into some money trouble, you see, and then I stupidly went to a bank for a loan, and—well, that didn't work out very well."

Michael was not exactly certain why Lucas was telling him this, but he did not want the young man to stop. Michael was fascinated to hear more of Mrs. Chase, more of what she was like when she was not wearing her armor of rules and propriety. What she worked for—what she loved. What her troubles were. He nodded encouragingly at Lucas.

"So I have to go back to Cambridge and study so one day *I* can take care of *her*. But I need your help."

"How can I possibly help? She thinks I have led you into wrong thinking and bad behavior by dismissing the rules."

Lucas frowned, looking so deeply young and very confused. "I have told her that is not so, that I misunderstood you! That it was all my own doing. And I will tell her that again. But I think something is wrong with Rosie, something besides me and my stupidity, and I cannot discover what it is. She always has to pretend to be so strong."

"Wrong? Is Mrs. Chase ill?" Michael said, alarmed.

"I don't think so, but she *is* tired. How could she not be, with me, and all those girls at her school to contend with? I think—no, I *know* that there are some financial troubles, and they are mostly my own fault. Since I cannot be here with her, someone has to keep an eye on Rosie, make sure she doesn't worry herself to death. Could *you* do it, Morley? Just for a while, until she goes back to the country."

"Me?" Michael sat back in his chair. Of course it would be no great hardship to watch Mrs. Chase; quite the opposite. The more he saw her, the more he was fascinated by her. Yet he could not imagine that she would welcome such attentions from him. Not yet, anyway. Not until he could persuade her of his finer qualities. "I doubt Mrs. Chase would allow me to, er, keep an eye on her."

Lucas laughed ruefully. "She *is* dashed stubborn, it's true. Yet I'm sure you could do it without her knowing. You like her, do you not?" There was an eagerness in Lucas's eyes, in his entire manner.

Like? That was such a tepid word for what Michael was coming to feel for her. "I admire Mrs. Chase, yes."

"I do not see how anyone could *not* admire Rosie! She's a brick. If you could just look in on her while she's in Town, take her about to museums and such. She likes dusty old places such as that. Perhaps you could even discover what is bedeviling her? There must be something besides money."

"I could do that, if Mrs. Chase would allow me to. I confess to a liking for dusty places myself."

Lucas gave him a relieved smile. "That is all I can ask. You are a good man, Morley, and I am sure my sister will come to see that, too. All this misunderstanding about rules and such will be as nothing once she gets to know you."

Lucas took his leave soon after that, but Michael sat in his chair long after it was full dark, and the glow of the lamps was his only light.

Keep an eye on Mrs. Chase. Oh, yes, he could certainly do that, and keep men like his so-called friend Will Beene away from her while he did it. And he would start by inviting her to the theater tomorrow evening.

Chapter Fourteen

"True friendship is one of life's greatest treasures."
A Lady's Rules for Proper Behavior, Chapter Three

*R*osalind was deep in delicious sleep, just clinging to the edges of a half-remembered dream, when she became aware that someone was sitting at her bedside, watching her intently.

She suddenly remembered that strange man she had seen watching the house, and she sat up with a terrified gasp—only to find Georgina perched on the edge of the bed, like a morning bluebird in her sky-colored dressing gown.

"Georgie!" she screamed. "You scared me out of my wits. What are you doing here so early? You never rise before ten at the least. Is something amiss?"

"Not a thing, as far as I know. I'm sorry I woke you," Georgina said, looking not in the least repentant. "But I thought you might want to see these, and you were sleeping ever so late. Late for you, anyway."

Rosalind, finally able to catch her breath, noticed what Georgina held on her lap. A bouquet of white roses and a small, ribbon-tied box. "Flowers? You had to wake me especially for that?" Rosalind wondered if she was still dreaming.

"Not just any flowers. They are from Lord Morley, as is the box. And I have not even peeped inside, though I am aching to know what is there!" She de-

posited the offerings on the counterpane next to
Rosalind.

Rosalind stared down at the flowers. Now she *knew*
she was still dreaming, if she was receiving gifts from
Lord Morley before the household was even awake.
She slowly reached out with one fingertip to touch the
blossoms, half expecting to feel the warmth of his skin
there. She felt only the cool lushness of a petal.

Georgina stretched out beside her, and for one moment Rosalind felt like a schoolgirl again. She and
Georgina and Elizabeth Everdean had often stayed up
late to talk and giggle, mostly over young men and
imagined romances. But she had never known anyone
like Lord Morley when she was fifteen. She had not
even dreamed there *could* be someone like him.

"Well?" Georgina prompted impatiently. "Aren't
you going to open the box?"

Rosalind slowly pulled at the end of the satin ribbon
and drew it off the box. She lifted the lid—and
laughed.

"What?" Georgina cried. "What is it?"

"Cakes," answered Rosalind.

Georgina scowled in disappointment. "Just cakes?
No emeralds or anything like that?"

"Certainly not. Even Lord Morley is not so wildly
improper as to send me emeralds. And cakes are fine
enough, when they are marzipan-frosted cakes from
Gunter's."

"So they *are* from Morley, then?"

"I believe so. No one else would be sending me
flowers and cakes." Rosalind was amazed that *Lord
Morley* would send gifts. She was hardly his usual sort,
she thought, remembering Lady Clarke and her daring, close-fitting gowns. But it was nice to receive them
all the same.

She took one of the tiny, luscious cakes and popped
it into her mouth. As she did this, she saw the neatly
folded note tucked among the sweets.

"My dear Mrs. Chase," it read. "I hope that you
enjoy these—they are Gunter's finest. And I hope they

recall to you our pleasant afternoon yesterday. Dare I hope you will allow me to escort you to the theater this evening? I have procured tickets to *The Merchant of Venice,* as my sister tells me you are very fond of Shakespeare. I will have my man call at Wayland House this afternoon for your answer."

Rosalind heard herself giggle—actually *giggle*!—and she pushed the paper back into the box.

But Georgina's eyes were sharp, and she saw the note before it disappeared amid the cakes. "What was that? A billet-doux?"

"Certainly not. It was merely a message stating that he—Lord Morley—hopes I enjoy the cakes, and asks if he might escort me to the theater this evening."

"The theater!" Georgina bounced up onto her knees in excitement. "Oh, how perfectly *splendid.* How delicious!"

"Delicious? It is Shakespeare. Most edifying and uplifting."

"Edifying and uplifting? Aren't you just Miss Butter Wouldn't Melt? You are such a sly puss, Rosie. Morley is sought after by every lady in the city, probably every lady in the *nation,* and here he is dangling after you. Of course it is delicious. It is marvelous!"

"It makes me feel queasy," Rosalind murmured.

Georgina dismissed this with a wave of her hand. "Naturally it would. There are no men like Morley in your quiet corner of the country, where you choose to bury yourself. You are one of the best people I know, Rosie—you always think of everyone but yourself, and you never see how lovely you truly are. You deserve a man like Morley. You deserve excitement, and love."

Love? Rosalind's bewildered gaze shot to the gloating Georgina, then fell back to the box of cakes. Was this terrible ache, this complete oversetting of her sensible, careful life—love? She did not know. She *could* not know. Perhaps it was just a surfeit of sugar in the morning. "How does a person know when it's really love, Georgie?"

Georgina gave her a smug, satisfied smile. "Oh, one just knows, Rosie. One just knows. I knew right away that Alex was the man for me, from the first moment I saw him. It just took him a little longer, the stubborn darling."

This bewildering conversation was interrupted by a soft knock at the door. A maid came into the room, and dropped a quick curtsy. "Beg your pardon, Your Grace, Mrs. Chase, but Mr. Allen Lucas is in the drawing room for Mrs. Chase."

Allen was here? Rosalind set aside the box and the flowers, and slid down out of the high bed. Practical family concerns had to push aside silly romantic flutterings for the moment. Allen had promised her he would go back to Cambridge—she prayed he was not in more trouble now. She deeply hoped she would not have to meet yet again with that reptilian banker.

"Tell Mr. Lucas I will be down in a few moments," she told the maid. The girl curtsied again, and hurried away.

Georgina watched from her perch at the foot of the bed as Rosalind pulled a morning gown and a pair of slippers from the wardrobe. "Do not think you have escaped me, Rosie," she sang out. "We *will* talk of this further. I want to know *everything* about you and Lord Morley. You are livening up my dull life."

Rosalind doubted very much that Georgina's life was ever dull, but she wished she herself could know *everything* about this situation, she thought as she sat down to pull on her stockings. But she feared she knew nothing at all. And she so hated that feeling.

Michael paused before raising the brass knocker of the Waylands's front door—and glanced up at one of the upper windows, sensing a gaze on him. Lady Elizabeth Anne stood there watching him, her long red ringlets falling over the bodice of her small velvet dressing gown. She waved to him and gave him a merry smile. He just had time to wave in return before a nursemaid came and fetched her away.

He laughed, and thought that a daughter of Mrs. Chase's would also appear very much like that, with red curls and china-doll skin. Would she also be dangerously precocious, like Elizabeth Anne, or proper and rule-following? Either way, it would be a very fortunate man indeed who fathered such a child.

And then it hit him, like a lightning strike from the gods. *He* wanted to be that father. He wanted to be the man who took Mrs. Chase—Rosalind, Rosie—into his arms and his bed every night; who came home to find a tiny, redheaded imp running down the stairs crying "Papa!" He wanted to buy his Rosie gowns of silk and satin and glittering jewels, to take his family to Italy and Greece and watch them playing in the sun and the sea. He wanted to write odes to red hair and blue eyes like the sky, to pink lips that pursed in an adorably proper way.

He had thought he just wanted to flirt with her, to enjoy teasing her out of her propriety and her rules. But, when he was not looking, it became more than that. So much more.

He was falling in love with her. But she still thought him a silly ass, a reckless poet who ruined her life by leading her brother into trouble with rule-breaking.

How could he show her that it was not true, that he was not that person she thought him? How could he even begin to persuade her of his finer qualities? Did he even *have* finer qualities? He was not sure. But at least she had agreed to this theater outing. That was a start.

The front door opened so suddenly that he was forced to take a step back. He did not even remember knocking, yet there stood the Waylands's butler, holding out a hand for Michael's cloak and hat.

"Lord Morley," the butler said. "Mrs. Chase is expecting you. She and Her Grace are in the drawing room, if you care to follow me."

Expecting him, was she? Michael thought as he stepped into the gilt and marble foyer. He could only hope that was truly so.

*   *   *

Rosalind peered one more time into the mirror, and smoothed the bodice and cap sleeves of her gown. She had worn one of her own garments this evening, her best gown of pale gray lutestring silk piped in black satin. It was a sort of armor; she felt protected in it, as she never could in Georgina's dashing, brightly colored creations. But she had left off her cap, instead anchoring her piled-up curls with onyx combs.

She touched one of those combs, and wished for one of those caps.

"No, you may not go upstairs and put on one of those hideous caps," Georgina called from over the high back of the settee where she lounged.

"I was not even thinking of caps!" Rosalind retorted. She dropped her hand down to her side.

"Of course you were." Georgina serenely turned over a page in the fashion paper she was reading. "Since I have become a mother I have learned to read minds. I know when Elizabeth Anne is plotting mischief, or when Sebastian has a fever—or when you want to put on a cap. But you are lovely just as you are, Rosie, even if you would not wear the green satin. Come and sit down while you wait for Lord Morley."

There was no time for sitting, though, or for going upstairs to fetch a cap. The drawing room door opened, and the butler announced, "Lord Morley, Your Grace."

And there he was, as handsome as could be in an evening coat of emerald green velvet, another cravat of daffodil yellow about his throat. A square-cut emerald winked in its crisp folds.

Rosalind was very glad she had *not* worn the green satin gown Georgina offered, for then she and Lord Morley would have looked like a walking Irish meadow together. Of course, no matter what she wore, no one would glance twice at *her* when they could look at him. He was like some dark, pagan god, and his beauty only increased when he smiled at her and gave her an elegant bow.

"Good evening, Duchess. Mrs. Chase. You are both very elegant tonight." His gaze lingered on Rosalind, warm and admiring.

She could think of nothing to say, not even the little politenesses she wrote about so often. Her throat was dry, closed.

Thanks heaven for Georgina, who never lost her social aplomb. She laughed and said, "You flatterer, Lord Morley! I look like an old ragpicker, since I am settled in for a quiet evening at home. But Rosalind *is* elegant, as always."

"Thank you for the compliment, Lord Morley," Rosalind finally managed to say. "You are too kind."

"Oh, I am merely truthful, Mrs. Chase. Shall we depart? I have heard that Kean is quite fine as Shylock, and it would be a shame to miss the opening curtain."

"Of course." Rosalind picked up her gray satin shawl and handed it to him. He swept an errant curl from the nape of her neck before slowly, ever so slowly, sliding the smooth fabric over her shoulders. His fingers lingered at her bare skin for just an instant longer than was proper.

Rosalind almost forgot to breathe. "I—I do so enjoy Shakespeare," she gasped.

"As do I," he answered, a hint of laughter in his brandy-dark voice. "And I think I will enjoy the old Bard of Avon tonight more than ever."

He stepped around to her side and offered her his arm. She smiled up at him, and slid her fingers over the rough softness of his velvet sleeve.

"Good night, you two!" Georgina called gaily as they left the drawing room. "Do not stay out too late."

The theater was crowded with merrymakers when Rosalind stepped into the box Lord Morley had reserved. Every box glittered with jewels and opera glasses and silks, though it seemed no one was paying heed to the pre-Shakespeare farce playing on the stage. The level of conversation and laughter was so high that Rosalind could not hear the dialogue at all.

Not that she could have paid it much heed, anyway. Not with Morley beside her.

The box was one of the smaller in the theater, so their gilt chairs were placed close together. Rosalind fussed with her shawl, and with taking her opera glasses from her reticule.

"Are these seats to your liking, Mrs. Chase?" he asked. "There was not much choice to be had when I went to procure tickets. It seems to be a fine vantage point, though."

"It is quite fine," answered Rosalind. Fine for people to see *them* anyway, she thought, watching as numerous gazes turned their way. She lifted her chin and ignored them, focusing her attention on the stage. "I have not been able to attend the theater as much as I would like since coming to Town. I was very happy to receive your invitation."

"Were you, Mrs. Chase?" he asked, his voice oddly intent. Almost as if he truly *cared* about her answer.

Rosalind glanced at him, but it was shadowed in their box. A ray of light slanted over his brow, his sharp cheekbone, but his eyes—the windows to his thoughts—were in darkness.

But she could not turn away.

"Oh, yes," she murmured. "I was. I did so enjoy our afternoon yesterday. Lady Violet is looking well. Sometimes, when she returns to the Seminary from her times at home, she seems rather—tired."

"She was excited to see you. You are her idol, you know. Everything with her is Mrs. Chase this and Mrs. Chase that. One could hardly blame her, of course."

Rosalind gave a startled laugh. "Her *idol*? I am a poor choice for that."

"No, indeed, Mrs. Chase. I think you are the finest choice she could have made."

"I am glad, of course, if I have been of some help to her. I become so very fond of the girls who pass through my school."

"You enjoy teaching, then?"

Rosalind relaxed a bit. Here was a topic she was truly comfortable with. "Oh, yes. Mr. Chase and I never were blessed with children. I suppose these girls are a bit like—well, like substitute daughters. I am fond of them. Most of them, anyway!"

"I envy you, Mrs. Chase, having a life's work you love so."

"Do you not love your own work, Lord Morley?" Rosalind asked in surprise. "Your poetry is so very glorious! You must put so much of yourself into it."

"Have you read my poetry, then?" he asked, that dark, intent note in his voice again.

"I—yes. A few poems." In truth, she had gone secretly to a bookseller when she first arrived in London and purchased all three volumes of his work. She found his verse intoxicating, exhilarating. Only someone who truly loved what he was doing could write so very passionately. "I found them to be—interesting."

"Interesting, eh?" He gave her a very pleased smile. "I am flattered, Mrs. Chase. And rather surprised you would bother with my piddling verses. I am hardly Shakespeare, as I am sure you have discerned."

"Just as your sister speaks often of me, my brother speaks of you. I was curious about his idol. And, speaking of my brother, I had a very interesting visit from him this afternoon."

"Did you, Mrs. Chase? I trust he is well."

"Very well. In fact, he has vowed to me that he is returning to Cambridge and will stay there. I wonder whatever could have inspired such a change of heart?" She peered closely at Morley. She knew very well what could have precipitated such a change—a man Allen admired giving him a stern talking-to. And she knew Allen had gone to Morley's lodgings yesterday afternoon.

But Lord Morley merely shrugged and grinned. "Lucas is not a bad young man, he is merely—young. He just needs to be nudged in the right direction."

"I am very grateful to anyone who can, as you say,

nudge him. I have had little luck in the past few years."

"I will always be happy to assist you in any way I can, Mrs. Chase. Any way at all."

She felt his hand touch hers, briefly but so very warmly, under the cover of a fold in her heavy skirt. And, much to her shock, Rosalind found herself pressing his hand in return.

"Friendship *and* theater tickets," she whispered. "Those are fine assistance indeed."

"Then, since we are friends, may I escort you to the Smith-Knightley ball tomorrow evening?" he whispered back.

"I would like that very much, Lord Morley," she replied, forgetting every rule she herself had written about demurely turning away invitations.

This fairy tale would all end soon enough. Why should she not enjoy it while it was happening?

She would enjoy every minute of it.

Wayland House was dark and quiet when Rosalind returned from the theater. The butler, who took her wrap and then melted back into the shadows, seemed to be the only living being in the marble silence.

Rosalind was grateful for the solitude. She had so very much to think about, to process in her own mind, to hug close to her heart after her splendid evening. She knew Georgina would want to find out every detail, but Rosalind did not think she could talk about it. Not just yet.

But as she walked down the corridor that led to her chamber, she saw that she was not alone in Wayland House after all. The door to Georgina's personal sitting room was half open, spilling golden firelight across the dark wood floor. Standing by the fireplace, silhouetted in the glow, were Georgina and her husband. They were locked in each other's arms, in a passionate kiss, Georgina's brilliant hair flowing over Alex's hands.

"My darling Georgie," he groaned, sliding his lips to her temple, her cheek.

"Alex," murmured Georgina, as she swayed closer to him.

Rosalind eased the door shut before they could realize they were being observed and went on her way. Her heart warmed at the knowledge that there *could* be such love in the world—and sparked with just a hint of envy.

Chapter Fifteen

"Always wear gloves when dancing; bare flesh
should never, ever touch bare flesh."
A Lady's Rules for Proper Behavior, Chapter Four

*T*he Smith-Knightley ball was every bit the crush
that the Portman soiree had been. People clad in
the first stare of fashion were crowded to the walls,
their laughter and conversation a thick cloud hovering
over the room, drowning out the lively dance music.
Couples swirled elegantly through a pavane, while observers
gossiped about the gowns and partners of others.
It was all a perfectly ordinary evening out for
the *ton*.

Yet Rosalind was more nervous than she had ever
been in her life. She had attended more routs and
fetes in her short time here in Town than ever before
in her life, and she had became rather accustomed to
them. Not exactly comfortable, yet she did not find
them unenjoyable by any means. They were—
interesting.

But she had never attended a ball on the arm of
Lord Morley. That made this evening an entirely different
proposition altogether.

Her silk-gloved fingers tightened on Morley's superfine sleeve as they waited outside the ballroom doors
for the Smith-Knightleys's butler to announce them.
This had seemed such a fine idea last night, when she
sat so close to him in the darkened magic of the the-

ater. She had even looked forward to it, when she looked into his dark eyes as he issued the invitation.

Now things felt so very different. Now that they were actually faced with a roomful of people—people who were avidly interested in everything the dashing Lord Morley did, people who had seen them together at Gunter's and in the theater. She was abandoning years of quiet living and perfect discretion on this portal. She had imagined it would be difficult.

It was harder than any imagining could have been.

Rosálind would have turned and run away, if Georgina and the duke were not standing right behind her, chatting and laughing as if this was an absolutely ordinary evening. They, and a few other couples who waited beyond them, blocked her exit utterly.

Rosalind turned back to face the ballroom doors, fidgeting with the skirt of her coral-colored silk gown. She peered down at it, watching the way the shimmering fabric draped and glistened in the candlelight. This dress was far more elaborate than anything she ever wore in her *real* life, sewn with golden spangles on the short, puffed sleeves and along the hem. She gained some superficial courage from its sparkle and flash.

"Are you sorry you came?" Morley whispered, leaning close to her. His cool breath stirred the loose curls at her temple.

Rosalind shivered at the sensations this evoked. Warm, unfamiliar, *tingling* sensations. "Of course not," she answered stoutly.

He grinned at her. "Liar."

Rosalind laughed. "I would *never* tell a falsehood. That would be most improper."

"Against the rules, eh?"

Her lips tightened at the mention, the reminder, of the rules. How could she have forgotten them so quickly, when they were such a large part of her life? Whenever she was with him, everything else just fell away. "Quite right."

They did not have time to say anything else. The

doors opened, and the butler took their names. "The Duke and Duchess of Wayland," he announced. "Mrs. Rosalind Chase. Viscount Morley."

On legs that seemed turned to water, Rosalind stepped into the ballroom. Her hand tightened on his arm. She no longer held onto him just for appearance's sake—she needed his strength to hold her up.

As she had expected, and feared, heads swiveled in their direction. She had a blurred impression of disappointed pouts on the faces of young ladies, the glint of raised quizzing glasses, waves of avid curiosity.

There was nothing for her to do but lift her chin, feign deepest disinterest, and keep moving into the crowd. At Lord Morley's side.

She was very glad for Georgina and her steady stream of inconsequential talk. "Oh, look over there, Rosalind. Isn't that Mrs. Strandling? We went to school with her, did we not? She should never wear that shade of green. Ah, champagne. Delightful. Do you care for a glass, Rosalind? Alex, darling?"

Rosalind stared intently at the pale, beckoning liquid, sparkling in crystal flutes on the footman's tray. The delicious drink called to her, but she knew she should not indulge. Champagne tended to make her giddy. The last thing she wanted to be tonight was *giddy*.

"Oh, no, not right now," she said.

"Mrs. Chase has promised me a dance," Morley told them. "I hear a waltz beginning, and she knows that is my favorite dance."

Rosalind knew no such thing—she did not think she had ever spoken two words about dancing with him. But the promise of occupation, of movement, of having something to concentrate on besides people's stares, was enticing indeed. "Of course," she said. "Thank you, Lord Morley. A waltz sounds very pleasant."

He led her onto the polished dance floor, and they took their place amid the assembled couples. When he put his hand on her waist, pulling her close, but

not so very close as to incite more talk, the gawking
crowd seemed to melt away. Rosalind heard no whis-
pers. The two of them were all alone in the teeming
crush, just as it had seemed they were last night in
the theater box. Nothing else mattered, not even the
fact that she had only practiced the waltz a few times,
in classes with the girls at her school.

She had no fears of making a fool of herself, of
being the object of gossip. Not when he stood so close
to her, smiling down at her.

"Are you quite all right?" he murmured. "You went
very white all of a sudden."

"All right?" she whispered back, thrown off balance
by his question.

"I should have realized how very interested people
would be when we appeared here together. I am so
accustomed to being speculated over that I scarcely
take note of it anymore. But you are not used to such
scrutiny. I'm sorry."

"It does not matter," Rosalind answered, and realized, with some degree of shock, that it truly did not.
She had lived all her life being careful, being always
so painfully proper. She was suddenly so deeply tired
of it all. She just wanted to dance, to forget, to have
fun—like everyone else. Like people who had no
school or wayward brother to worry over.

Tomorrow would be soon enough for her to worry
again. Tonight, she would just dance.

"Good," he said. "I am very glad to hear it."

She tightened her clasp on his hand, and closed her
eyes as the music reached its lively opening beats.
They swayed together, and swung into the dance.

This was like no dance she had ever known before.
Dancing classes with the girls, local assemblies with
her husband—they were nothing like this. Rosalind's
feet, which she had always hated as being too big,
seemed dainty and graceful as they glided across the
floor. She hummed along with the lilting tune, and
turned and twirled effortlessly in his arms. She felt—
why, she felt *beautiful*! She felt desirable and flirta-

tious and merry, as if deciding she would leave her real life behind until tomorrow had freed her to be someone else.

"You are a wonderful dancer, Mrs. Chase," he said, turning her in a spin that sent her skirts flaring in a graceful arc.

"I help the girls with their dancing lessons at the Seminary," she answered. "So I have had a great deal of practice. Not in waltzing, though."

His hand at her waist drew her closer, so close she could smell the faint, spicy scent of his soap, the starch from the folds of his dark blue cravat. He was so close she could lean her cheek against the curve of his jaw, feel the satin of his hair on her skin.

She leaned back a bit, trying to escape that intoxicating fragrance. But his heat reached after her, beckoning her back to him.

He did not loosen his clasp. His eyes were heavy-lidded as he stared down at her, dark, serious, intent.

"I hope they do not end up using their lessons in quite this way," he said hoarsely. "At least not until they are a good deal older."

"In what way?" she asked, mesmerized by his gaze. "This is all quite proper."

"Oh, yes, of course. Quite proper." They danced past half-open glass doors, and, before Rosalind could even blink, he twirled her out of them onto a night-shadowed terrace. They ended behind a tall, sheltering bank of potted plants.

"Proper—until now," he whispered. And then he kissed her.

Rosalind gasped against his lips, shocked at the feel of them, the softness, at the suddenness of the caress—at the feelings that crashed inside her heart. For a flash, her old, sensible self shrieked in horror, but that old Rosalind was quickly submerged beneath the sweetness, the heat of the kiss.

Her lips parted, and she twined her arms about his neck, leaning into him. She trembled as if in a wind-swept storm, and it was frightening. Almost as frightening as it was delicious. Part of her wanted to step away, to be in control again, but a larger part, that now *was* in control, knew that this was precisely where she wanted to be. Where she had to be. In truth, she had longed for his kiss, his touch, ever since he had come to her in her office at the Seminary and offered her a cup of tea.

Her arms tightened around his neck, her fingers seeking the waves of his hair that fell over his velvet collar. The locks clung to her silk gloves, warm and living through the thin fabric. He pulled back, as if surprised, and stared down at her, breathing fast.

Rosalind blinked open her eyes. Everything was blurred around the edges, soft and hot. He was so close she could see the flecks of amber in his dark eyes, the way his hair, disarranged by her fingers, tumbled over his brow.

"Rosalind," he murmured. "Rosie. You are so beautiful." One of his magical fingers trailed down her cheek, traced her lips.

She? Beautiful? She had never thought so before; she was too tall, too redheaded, too freckled. In his arms, at this moment, she was beautiful. He made it so.

"Not as beautiful as you, Lord Morley."

He smiled, and his hands slid up to cradle her face. "My name is Michael."

"Michael," she whispered. The name was dark and sweet, like a cup of chocolate, a sip of brandy, in her mouth. "Michael."

He groaned, and bent his head to kiss her again. She fell back against the wall of the house. The stone was cold and sharp through the thin silk of her gown, but she scarcely noticed it when Lord Morley—*Michael*—leaned in close to her. His lips slid from hers along the line of her throat, down to her bare shoulder.

"So sweet," he whispered, the words reverberating against her skin. She felt his hand on the sleeve of her gown, drawing it down . . .

A ripple of loud laughter pierced the haze of her passion. Suddenly, the wall at her back was hard and cold again, the hand on her shoulder shocking. With a sharp intake of breath, she drew away, hitting her head with an audible thud on the wall. Her hands fumbled against his chest, pushing him back.

Michael stumbled away, the expression on his face as dazed as she herself felt. His hands slowly fell away from her, and he raked his fingers through his hair. He was dark and tousled.

Rosalind closed her eyes tightly, shutting out the dangerously attractive sight of him. Never in all her life had she done something as shocking as kiss a man on a public terrace. Anyone could have seen them! And, if she was truly honest with herself, they had been doing rather more than kissing there.

She had spent so very long condemning her brother's foolish behavior. But she was far more imprudent than he had been. She had broken so many rules tonight, she could never be redeemed. How could she ever look at her students again, ever teach them proper behavior, without knowing herself for the hypocrite she was?

Yet, somehow, she could not be truly, deeply sorry. She could not regret kissing Michael. For those few, precious moments, she had felt more *alive* than she ever had before.

Had the rules ever made her feel like that? She had to admit that they had not.

She moaned in confusion, and reached up to press her hands against the threatening headache. In the midst of all this turmoil, she felt a soft touch on her arm. Michael drew her sleeve back up to her shoulder, gently, tenderly.

Rosalind opened her eyes to peek up at him. He also seemed confused, bewildered, pained—but he smiled at her, a wry, rueful grin. "Oh, Rosalind. Mrs. Chase. I am so sorry. I never meant . . ."

He never meant—what? To kiss a tall, awkward schoolmistress on a terrace? To almost be caught? A sour pang of disappointment added to Rosalind's chill, to her disillusionment. She turned away, patting and pulling at her hair. She wished ardently for one of her caps.

"It is quite all right," she said tightly. "There was no harm done. Perhaps we should go inside? I am sure Georgina will be looking for me."

Actually, Georgina was probably hoping that something very like this—or rather, like their kiss—was happening, and she would not be looking for Rosalind for quite a while. But for Rosalind the thought of a crowded ballroom was a haven for once. There, she would have no time to think of all this, whatever *this* was.

"If that is what you wish, of course," Michael said softly. She heard the sinuous rustle of cloth as he straightened his coat. "But I want to tell you . . ."

"Later. Please." Rosalind simply could not hear him right now, not while she was so confused. Not while the voices of the new arrivals on the terrace were coming ever closer. "We will speak later, yes?"

"Of course," he said. "But I will hold you to that—Rosalind."

He stepped to her side, and offered her his arm. Rosalind slid her hand onto his sleeve, careful not to cling too tightly, to feel the warm strength of his muscles and bone.

As they walked past the group of people, she heard a woman say, "Is that not Lord Morley? But who is that with him? I heard he was at the theater last night with some unknown redhead. Is that she?"

One of the men with her answered, "Perhaps so, m'dear. But doesn't *A Lady's Rules* say 'A lady will never walk alone with a gentleman after dark, or risk great harm to her reputation'?"

The entire group laughed tipsily, and Rosalind cringed. That was just one of the many rules she had broken this evening.

And she had the distinct feeling that it was not the last she would break before all of this was finished.

*   *   *

Michael moved through the crowd with Mrs. Chase on his arm, stopping to speak to friends, to bow to matrons, and smile and laugh. Yet it was as if he watched the entire scene from very far away, not participating at all. He had been through routs like this dozens, hundreds of times before, and could make all the correct postures, but he was not aware of them at all. He only felt the light pressure of her hand on his arm, the warmth of her at his side.

She also did everything that was proper, making all the correct responses and gestures. No one could possibly see the distraction in her eyes, the solemn downturn at the corners of her rose pink lips. No one except him.

He watched her as they traversed the edge of the ballroom. Mrs. Chase—*Rosalind*. Despite her solemnity, her stillness, she was quite the most beautiful woman in the room. The most beautiful woman in all of London. Her hair shone like the red and gold fire of dawn, caught up with coral-tipped combs and falling along the white column of her neck. She seemed serene, assured, as she took in the room with her sky blue eyes, but there, in their depths, he saw her uncertainty, her shyness.

She was as affected by their kiss as he was. He still trembled deep inside from the unexpected force of their passion, from the desire, the raw *need,* that had seized him when he took her in his arms. Never had a simple kiss affected him so deeply! There had been nothing in the world but her, her perfume, her lips beneath his, her arms around his neck, drawing him ever closer to her.

Now, as he peered down at her in the color and flash of the ballroom, he knew the truth, the truth he had only suspected when he called on her at Wayland House yesterday. He loved her. He loved his sister's stiff, proper, rule-following teacher! And he had loved her ever since he saw her alone in her office. Even then, he had sensed the bright fire beneath her re-strained coolness, and it drew him in.

He *loved* her! After all the years of writing of pas-sion and longing, of searching for it so desperately in his own life, he had finally found it where he would have never thought to look.

He wanted to shout his feelings to all the world, to seize Rosalind by her slender waist and twirl her about until they were both dizzy with laughter and joy. He could hardly do that in front of the entire *ton*, though. Even he had to follow some rules. But he did reach for her hand, drawing her around to face him. They stood still in a quiet corner, slightly apart from the social fray.

She blinked up at him, as if surprised by their sud-den stillness. "Lord Morley?"

He wished she would call him by his given name. He longed to hear it in her voice, hear her whisper *Michael*. "When can I see you again?" he asked.

"You—wish to see me again?"

Had she so soon forgotten their kiss? How could she think he would *not* want to see her after that? "Of course I do. Tomorrow? We could go for a drive in the park, early, before the fashionable hour."

She flicked an uncertain glance over her shoulder, back at the crowd. She opened her mouth, and closed it again. Her fingers tightened on his for one moment before she drew her hand away and took a step back. He had never seen the cool, collected Mrs. Chase so discomposed before.

So she was *not* immune to him. But he feared she *was* about to refuse his invitation, and he tried to gather his arguments to persuade her to agree. He wanted so much to see her again, away from this blasted crowd. He *needed* to see her.

He had no need to argue with her, though. She slowly nodded, and said, "Yes. A drive would be— most agreeable. I have some things I would like to tell you, Lord Morley. Important things I think you ought to know."

He smiled at her, amazed by the rush of relief and anticipation. He *would* see her again! They would be together in the comparative quiet of the park, close to each other on the seat of his phaeton. As for whatever it was she had to tell him—well, it could be nothing so dreadful that they could not talk it over together. Could it?

As he took her arm again and they turned to resume their promenade about the ballroom, he saw two familiar figures coming in the doors. Mr. Gilmore and Lord Carteret, without Mr. Lucas tonight. So the young pup had kept his promise to go back to university after all.

Gilmore noticed Michael standing there with Mrs. Chase, and pointed them out to Carteret. Carteret gave Michael a smirk, and an elaborately polite bow. "*The rules,*" he mouthed, and he and Gilmore turned away in laughter.

Well, Michael thought ruefully. So he had some things to tell Mrs. Chase, as well.

Chapter Sixteen

"A lady should never ride unchaperoned with a gentleman in the park."
—*A Lady's Rules for Proper Behavior*, Chapter Nine

The room was dim, shadowed, with rich red velvet draperies over the windows, hanging from the bedstead. The scent of wine, flowers, and woodsmoke lingered in the cool air. The only sounds were the crackling flames in the grate—and a man's husky whisper.

"Rosalind," he murmured. "You are so beautiful. So glorious."

His kiss, light as a butterfly's wings, moved down her throat, over her shoulder. His fingers drew her thin silk gown down her arms.

Her limbs were heavy, flooded with a languid warmth. Rosalind leaned back on satin pillows, and opened her eyes to see Michael smiling lazily down at her . . .

Rosalind sat straight up in bed, gasping. "It was a dream," she whispered. "Just a silly dream."

But a silly dream that left her trembling. She rubbed her hands over her face, and pushed back the unruly curls that had escaped from her careful plait. It had felt so very real, that dream. Not just the sensations, but the emotions.

Emotions she was not sure what to do with.

Rosalind pushed back the bedclothes and slid off

the bed to the floor. She padded on her bare feet over to the window, which she pushed open to the night. She closed her eyes to savor the cool breeze on her flushed face.

When she opened them again, she felt calmer, yet still unsettled. The city was quiet at this hour, with the barest tinges of a pale gray predawn light just peeking over the horizon. Everyone was home from the night's revels, tucked up safely in their beds. Soon, very soon, it would be full light, and in only a few hours Michael—Lord Morley—would be here to take her for that drive.

Rosalind groaned. How could she face him after such a dream? How could she face him, knowing how she truly wanted him? How she—cared for him?

Loved him.

Yes. There it was. She had fallen in love with him. Truly, she was the most pathetic woman in London. Perhaps in all of England.

Rosalind had never in her life been a romantic sort. She had never had the time, between looking after her family, running the school, writing her books. There had never been a chance to sigh over poetry, to wax sentimental over flowers and moonlight and handsome young men. She had cared for her husband, true, but their marriage had been above all an eminently sensible match. His touch, his gaze, had never made her burn or tremble . . .

. . . as Michael's did. There was nothing sensible there! He was so very wrong for her—too young, too highly placed in Society, too wild and romantic. For heaven's sake, the man kissed her on terraces where anyone could come upon them! Kissed her with a fervor, a passion, she had never before dreamed could truly exist.

This was madness. It was hopeless. A man like that could have no serious ideas of a woman like her. She was a prudish schoolmistress.

Yet she did not *feel* like a prudish schoolmistress any longer. Not when she was with him, or even when she just thought about him. She felt young, and giddy, and very silly. The old patterns, the old ways of thinking no longer fit in her heart. Michael had proven himself to be more, much more than she had first thought him. He *was* romantic, but he was also kind-hearted and steady, with a lovely consideration for his sister. He was a man she could almost begin to trust.

Could she herself also not be more than she had once thought? The old Mrs. Chase would never have dreamed of confiding in someone, especially a man, about her troubles. The new Rosalind wanted to tell Michael all, everything about her school, her books. She longed to put her head on his shoulder, feel his arms about her, and know, even if only for one moment, that she was not alone.

But she was scared. So scared that it chilled her heart.

Rosalind pushed her hair back from her neck, holding the heavy plait away from her flushed skin. For the first time in her life, she just did not know what to do.

Michael reached for a cravat—and paused. The cloth was of a sky blue color, a perfectly starched length of cloth just waiting for him to wrap it about his throat. Usually this was one of his very favorite colors, and it went perfectly with his silver brocade waistcoat. Today, it made him hesitate.

It made him wonder what Mrs. Chase would think of the color.

He could not remember when he had last considered what another person would think about his attire. Perhaps when his mother had been alive; she had been such a fashion plate, and had taken such delight in her child's early sartorial choices. But never since. People's opinions just did not matter.

He wanted to see the light of admiration, even of desire, in Rosalind's eyes when she saw him—eyes that were almost the color of this cloth. The light had been there last night, he was sure of that. He wanted to see it again more than he had ever wanted anything before in his life.

And Rosalind did not approve of the least hint of gaudiness in her attire. He considered reaching for a white cravat instead, something simple and stark, like a clergyman might wear. And *dull*. So very dull. He was *not* a curate, after all. His blue, and pink, and yellow cravats were a part of him, just as his writing was. Rosalind had seemed to like his colored cravat last night.

He tied it in a neat, stylish whorl, and speared it with a pearl-headed pin. As he turned away to reach for his dark blue superfine coat, his gaze fell on the papers that littered his desk. The sheets were stained and blotted with ink, some of them torn in deepest frustration. They were the beginnings of a poem he had started in the fevered depths of the night.

He could not sleep when he returned from the ball, could not stop the wild swirl of his thoughts, his emotions. They were tangled, confused, and he tried to sort them out the only way he knew how—by writing.

He picked up the top paper, the closest he had come to a final version. It was still far from perfect, but he *did* like the title—"A Kiss by Moonlight." Perhaps, one day, when it was polished properly, he would give it as a gift to Rosalind. Then she would know his feelings for her in a way that no spoken words could express.

Michael laughed, and tossed the poem back down onto the desk. Maybe by then he would know what those feelings were himself.

Right now, he only knew that that one kiss had affected him in ways he had never known before. No other woman, no matter how beautiful, how passionate, could compare to his tall, redheaded schoolmistress.

And he could not wait until he saw her again.

He caught up his hat and walking stick, and ran down the stairs to where his manservant waited with the phaeton.

* * *

"Lord Morley is calling for Mrs. Chase, Your Grace," the Waylands's butler announced.

"Thank you," Georgina said, and calmly turned the page of her book.

Rosalind, though, felt no such serenity. She dropped the embroidery she had not really been working on and leaped to her feet. Surely he was early! This could not yet be time for their drive.

She glanced wildly to the clock on the fireplace mantel. It was indeed the scheduled time for their outing, and she had no opportunity to go upstairs and change her gown again.

Her hands flew to her hair, which Georgina's lady's maid had arranged in a stylish tumble of curls. "Perhaps I should . . ." she began.

"No, Rosie!" Georgina interrupted sternly. "Your hair looks lovely. You mustn't change it." She put aside her book, and came to draw Rosalind's hands down before she could ruin the coiffure. "You look lovely, and you are going to have a splendid time this afternoon."

Rosalind left off with her hair, and plucked at the lace trim on the sleeves of her mulberry-colored carriage dress. "Will I?"

"Yes," Georgina said firmly. "You will drive in the park, and forget all about your book and your silly brother. What is wrong with you, Rosie? I have never seen you so—so *fidgety* before."

Rosalind did not know what was wrong with her.

There was no time to figure it out, though, for the butler was ushering Lord Morley—Michael—into the drawing room.

The park was not yet crowded, it being too early to be truly fashionable. The green spaces were mostly peopled by children with their watchful nannies, footmen walking pampered dogs, and couples who wanted a modicum of privacy.

Just like Lord Morley and herself, Rosalind realized

with a start of surprise. She had never thought to find herself seeking a quiet corner with a handsome young man, just as she had never imagined driving through a London park in a dashing phaeton, wearing a fashionable bonnet. The unlikelihood of this whole scenario happening to *her* made her laugh aloud.

Michael turned to her, one brow raised inquiringly. "Something amusing, Mrs. Chase?"

"Oh, yes," Rosalind answered. She felt oddly giddy, despite what she had to tell him today. These few moments in the springtime sunlight were unlike any she had ever known before or was likely to know again. All too soon, it would be vanished, like a sweetly remembered dream, and she would be back in her office at the Seminary wearing her caps and planning the new term. There was precious little romance there, amid all her cherished safety.

She should enjoy these moments while she had them, and come away knowing she had been honest with him. Honest about *some* things—she would tell him about *A Lady's Rules* and perhaps even her troubles over Allen and his loans. After all, he had truly proven to be a help with her brother, and seemed to have given up his utter hostility to the rules. But she would never, *could* never, tell him of her new feelings for him. Her desire to look foolish only went so far.

"This whole afternoon, no, this whole time in Town, has been amusing," she said. "It has all been so very unexpected. I will have something to remember when I return to the Seminary."

"Must you return there very soon?" he asked. He drew up the phaeton at the edge of a small pond, where they could watch ducks paddling by and children playing with their toy boats.

Rosalind sighed, both at the loveliness of the scene and knowledge of how quickly she would have to leave it. "Yes, quite soon. The new term will be starting, and I have to make sure all will be in preparation when the girls return."

"Violet will miss you very much," he said, his voice hoarse.

She dared not look at him, not directly. She feared all her emotions could be seen in her eyes. So she watched his gloved hand as he wrapped the reins about it. "But I will see her very soon, surely. Unless your father decides to end her enrollment. I do think . . ." She broke off, unable to say more.

Michael's free hand reached out suddenly to touch her arm. His clasp was warm through the muslin of her sleeve. Rosalind stared up at him, startled.

"You care about my sister, do you not, Mrs. Chase?" he said.

"Of course I do. Lady Violet has such a sweetness about her, I do not see how anyone could *not* care about her," Rosalind said. She did *not* tell him of the baby she had once lost, early in her marriage, and how she sometimes fancied that, had the child been a girl, she would have been a bit like Violet. Kind-hearted, sunny, pretty. That would sound too silly and sentimental, if said aloud. It was a secret of her own heart—one of many.

His hand slid away from her arm, and she found she missed his reassuring warmth. "Then Violet will be fine. She admires you so very much. I hope you will always stand as her friend, once she has left your school."

That seemed to be a sign that she had to tell him now—tell him some of those secrets she held. *You must begin as you mean to go on,* she told herself. And she meant to go forward in honesty now. She turned to face him, and blurted out, "*We* are friends, are we not?"

He seemed startled, but also very pleased. He gave her a slow smile, and said, "I hope we are. I would like so much to be your friend, Mrs. Chase, though I fear we started on the wrong foot. I behaved like a lout on that first day I came to see Violet at your school, and I fear I have not always been the greatest of gentlemen toward you since. I hope we can begin again?"

"Exactly!" Rosalind cried in relief that he understood her—understood her thus far, anyway. She feared that anyone as liberal-minded as he was might not understand her authorship of the *Rules*. "And friends—true friends—are honest with one another, correct?"

His smile dimmed a bit, but he nodded. "Yes."

"Then, as your friend, I must tell you something about myself."

Michael laughed. There seemed a strange mixture of disbelief and relief in the sound, with a tincture of light mockery that made her frown. This was a *serious* business! He rubbed his gloved hand along his jaw, and said, "You have dark secrets, Mrs. Chase? I can scarcely wait to hear them."

Rosalind turned away from him, blindly watching the people strolling along the edge of the pond. "I never said they were dark. I am not ashamed of them. They are simply the sort of matters that true friends share."

"Very well, then, Mrs. Chase. What are these—matters? I do truly want to hear them."

She took a deep, steadying breath, and folded her hands in her lap to keep them from shaking—and to hold herself down, so she would not leap from the phaeton and run away. "I had a very specific reason for coming to London, you see. And it was not just to visit my friend. It—well, it had to do with you, in a way."

"With me?"

"Yes. You see, Lord Morley, I wrote *A Lady's Rules for Proper Behavior,* and I had heard that you were breaking them all over the place. I had to find out for myself, because . . ." Rosalind broke off before she told him all about Allen's debts and her financial woes. One confession at a time seemed quite sufficient. She closed her eyes, and waited for his reaction.

His reaction was—silence. The other noises around

them, of children laughing, water splashing, wheels grinding on the pathway, were amplified in the strange quiet.

Slowly, uncertainly, Rosalind opened her eyes and glanced over at Michael.

His handsome face was utterly expressionless as he stared straight ahead. Then, as she watched, he began to laugh. At first it was a strange, startled chuckle, but it quickly became a deep, rollicking guffaw. He bent over, clutching at his sides as if they ached with so much laughter. The horses shifted restlessly, and children turned to stare at them.

Well! Rosalind thought with a huff. She turned away from him again. Here she had told the man one of her deepest secrets, and what did he do? He laughed. *Laughed!*

She was not sure what to do now. She was not much accustomed to being laughed at.

"It is not so funny as all that," she murmured. "Many people think I have important advice to impart."

She felt his touch on her arm, gentle yet insistent, and she stared down to see his dark glove against the lace of her sleeve. She did not yet dare peer up at his face, for fear of what she might see there. She did not think she could face ridicule right now. Not from him. Not when she had dared to let herself begin to feel close to him.

"My dear Mrs. Chase—Rosalind," he said. His voice was thick with his laughter, but there was no hint of mockery. He sounded beseeching. "Please forgive my laughter. That was unspeakably rude of me. No doubt against several rules."

So he *was* making fun of her! Rosalind tried to shrug off his hand, but his clasp was too strong. "Really, Lord Morley . . ."

"No, no, I am sorry. It is just that I feel so foolish for not guessing this before. It all makes such perfect sense."

Rosalind relented just a bit, ceasing her struggle to pull away. "What does?"

"How very proper you are, how insistent on following the rules. How you make certain every girl at your school has a copy of the book and learns to follow them, as well."

"I do *not* make the girls read the book simply because I wrote it. It is very important that they follow rules for proper behavior in Society, so that nothing ill befalls them because of their youth and inexperience. There are many unscrupulous young men who would take advantage of that."

"I know that you believe all that, Rosalind, and I admire you for it. Even a pagan like myself should behave properly, eh?" His hand slid down her arm to her fingers, which he lifted to his lips for a lingering kiss.

Rosalind shivered at the warm-cold sensations of that kiss, at the prickles of delight that went down to her very toes. He was indeed a pagan, a veritable Dionysus who tempted her to fall to his depths, to take off her shoes and run through the warm grass. To lie back in the golden glow of the sun and bask in kisses . . .

No! She could not think such things. Not right now. She removed her hand from his clasp, and placed it back on her lap. "Even pagans must behave with civility now and then, Lord Morley. Perhaps I will convert you yet."

"Before *I* can convert *you*?" He leaned closer, and whispered warmly in her ear, "Neither of us were thinking of the rules last night on that terrace, were we?"

Rosalind felt a flood of red heat spread from her cheeks, down her neck into her very soul. That was verily the truth. The rules had been the very last thing she was thinking of last night. All she had been thinking of was *him,* his taste, his feel.

"A gentleman would not bring up such a thing," she whispered back. She felt like such a ninny saying a prissy thing like that, but it was all she could think of. Her mind could not recall such mundane things as words and string them together in ways that made sense.

"Ah, well. I think we have established that I am not a true gentleman." He sat back lazily in the phaeton seat, one arm casually stretched along behind her shoulders. "But I hope I do not have an evil heart. I would never wish harm to you, Rosalind, and I apologize if my actions have hurt you in any way. Both last night, and in my dealings with your book."

Rosalind studied him closely. His dark eyes, usually alight with some mischief or delight, were uncharacteristically somber, his sensual lips downturned at the corners. He seemed truly sincere in his apology. "Thank you, Lord Morley."

"And, since you have been so very honest with me, I have a confession of my own to make."

A confession of his own? Rosalind felt the sudden chill of apprehension. Surely any confession of his would be far more scandalous than any of hers could be! "What is it you wish to tell me, Lord Morley?"

"First, that you should cease to call me Lord Morley. It seems ridiculous, when we are to know each other's deepest secrets. My name, as you well know, is Michael."

She nodded slowly, but in her mind she resolved to wait until *after* she heard his confession to decide what she would call him.

"It is really rather funny when you think about it," he said, with an attempt at his usual careless grin. "And it makes me feel quite foolish, like some bored schoolboy."

A schoolboy? That was one thing Rosalind would *never* think to compare him to. But now she fairly itched to know what his secret could be. She gave him what she hoped was an encouraging nod.

"One evening, at my club, I saw your brother and two of his friends, Lord Carteret and Mr. Gilmore. I believe you know them?"

Those two loobies. "Oh, yes. I know them."

"We were talking, and the conversation came around to *A Lady's Rules.* Your rules."

"What about them?"

"Oh, just how they are everywhere, and everyone is so very eager to follow them. You see, I fear the young men had been tossed out of a rout because of some small infraction of the rules. I stated that that did not seem like fair dealing, and someone—I believe it was Carteret—proposed a small wager. Since I had imbibed rather freely of some excellent port that evening, and was feeling rather out of sorts, I agreed."

A wager. Rosalind did not like the sound of that. Wagers always seemed to cause trouble, especially for her brother. She frowned down at her clenched hands. "What sort of a wager?"

He shifted uneasily on the seat. "That some people need not follow all the rules in order to be accepted, even admired, in Society. In truth, I have no excuse for doing such a thing! I was simply tired of seeing people like Violet behaving like automatons. Yet if I had known that this was *your* book, I never would have spoken about it."

Rosalind sat in silence for a long moment, absorbing all this strange—nay, ridiculous—information. So this was why her sales had fallen, the popularity of her rules waned, because of a wager. She could scarcely believe it. "So it was quite all right to do harm to someone when you did not know whose rules they were?"

"No!" he protested vehemently. "Of course not. I simply never considered that A Lady was a real person, with real needs associated with this book. Now I see that I was wrong about that. And I see what Lucas meant when he came to me . . ."

What Allen meant! Rosalind swung around to face him. "What did Allen come to you for? What did he say? I knew he wanted to visit you before returning to school, but surely he did not tell you . . ."

Michael held up his hand, as if to fend off her rapid-fire questions. "Nothing very great, I assure you! He was simply worried about you, and feeling ashamed of himself. He came to talk to me about his returning to Cambridge. He felt sorry for causing you trouble."

Rosalind sank back a bit against the seat cushions. She rarely allowed her temper to get the best of her—she would not let it now, no matter how much she wanted to hit him over the head with her reticule. "Tell me exactly what you and my brother spoke of."

"He simply told me he had been having some—difficulties lately, and he feared their effect on you. He told me he has a few debts, and you had been worried about them."

"And what did you tell him?"

"I simply tried to be his friend, to reassure him that these matters can be resolved, that no lives need be ruined over them. I certainly did not encourage him in running up those debts in the first place. Please believe me, Rosalind, I want only to help your brother—and you."

Rosalind gave him a short nod. She knew he *meant* no harm. They had come to know each other better in these last few days, and she knew he had no evil in his soul. But he *did* have mischief, and he did not realize that his very behavior, his very presence at that club, could influence young men like Allen.

"I know that you want to help," she conceded. "Allen is young, though, and impressionable. He should not be prattling about our private family business. I'm sorry he burdened you, especially when you were so very busy breaking the rules."

"He did not *burden* me!" Michael protested. "And I told you I was sorry about the blasted rules. They don't matter. Please, Rosalind. Let me help you, if I can. Let me make some amends for my foolish behavior."

Rosalind was confused and suddenly very tired. Her head was beginning to ache, with that telltale throb over her left eye. She did not know *how* she felt about all of this—about Michael, about all of the whirlwind changes her life had encountered in the last few days. She was used to quiet and order, not wagers and confessions and idiot kisses! She needed to be alone, to think.

"I would like to return to Wayland House now, please," she said.

He opened his mouth, as if to protest, but then shook his head. His fist clenched on the reins. "Of course, Mrs. Chase. But will you at least think of what I have said? Think of forgiving me?"

"Of course I will think about what you have said," Rosalind answered. It was all she could say; her head ached in earnest now.

He nodded shortly, and pulled on the reins to guide the horses out of their shady shelter back into the bright light of day.

That had not gone as badly as he feared it might, Michael thought, as he steered the phaeton back onto the pathway. Yet neither had it gone all that well.

Rosalind was the most difficult woman he had ever met. Most ladies let him know, through means both subtle and decidedly not so, that they either appreciated his interest or just wished he would go away. With Rosalind, he was never sure. She was always so very still, so serene, so blasted *polite*. But sometimes her eyes would flash at him with a brilliant light, or she would stiffen in a fury of temper all too quickly contained.

Or she would kiss him with heated passion on a terrace.

He had known, from the time he encountered her alone in her office, that there was much more to her than what she showed the world. Their time together in these last few days had only proven him right. She was fiercely protective of her brother, of her school and the girls who attended classes there. She was intent on being respectable and proper at all times, that was true, but there was also a yearning for *life* deep inside of her. He saw it in her eyes when they ate ices

at Gunter's and watched the actors at the theater. She
longed for excitement, for wonder, even though she
would not admit that to herself.

She made Michael want to give her all of that excitement, to show her all the beauties that life and the
world could hold. He wanted to share it all with her—
and more.

He had guessed some of the secrets of her heart, it
was true. Yet he had *not* guessed the one she had
confessed today. He had never supposed, even for a
moment, that she was the author of *A Lady's Rules*.

Michael almost laughed aloud now to think of it! He
should have known. It now seemed so very obvious.
Rosalind was so intent on following those rules, on
making certain that everyone else did, too. She had
even given *him* a copy! But he had always supposed
A Lady to be some elderly spinster, dreaming up dictates in her stuffy chamber and sending them out for
Society to be crazed over. He had never pictured her
as a beautiful redhead.

Michael glanced over at her now. She sat beside
him on the phaeton seat, her posture perfectly
straight, hands folded in her lap, a pleasant half-smile
on her face. He felt a great rush of pride for her, for
her ingenuity in writing that book in the first place,
for her courage in going out in Society to defend her
principles. He himself found a creative saving grace in
his poetry; she had found it in manners, and she had
done what almost no one else could do—she had
made the *ton* behave.

No matter how much he had, and still did, hate
mindless rule-following, he had to admire her for that.
And for a hundred other things, as well.

He *had* to make her forgive him for that stupid
wager! He had to make her see that it meant nothing,
had to undo any damage he might have caused. He
had only just found her. It would kill him to lose
her now.

He turned the phaeton around a corner and down
the street where Wayland House sat. They had only

a few more moments. He had to secure her promise that he would see her again.

"Will you be at Violet's soiree tomorrow evening?" he asked, slowing the horses to a mere crawl.

She glanced at him from the corner of her eye. "Of course. The duchess and Lady Emily also plan to attend. Lady Violet seemed so very excited about the event."

"So she is. Our father rarely deigns to entertain, and as Violet is not yet 'out' she must take every advantage of any occasion. I would not wish to excite your anticipation about the amenities, though—our father's cook concentrates only on what might charitably be called 'plain fare.' Trifles and cutlets and such."

Rosalind laughed quietly. It was a beautiful sound, one he could have listened to for hours and hours. He would stand on his head, make funny noises, wear jester's motley, do handsprings—*anything* to make her laugh.

Unfortunately, he had to keep his hands on the reins to keep them from crashing. But her one small laugh had already given him immeasurable hope.

"Oh, I can enjoy the splendors of haute cuisine every day at Wayland House, with Georgina's French chef," she said. "I look forward to your sister's company, and to meeting your aunt, Lady Minerva Fielding. I am sure it will be an enjoyable evening."

"If you are there, it shall be." They drew up outside Wayland House. Michael thought he saw a curtain twitch at one of the upstairs windows, but he could not be sure. Probably Lady Elizabeth Anne spying again.

"Thank you for the drive, Mich—Lord Morley," Rosalind said, excruciatingly polite. "The park was lovely."

Michael could not let her go like this, with a proper thanks she would give to any stranger. Boldly, he took her hand, holding the warmth of it against the lapel of his coat, uncaring that she would feel the powerful thrum of his heart.

Rosalind stiffened, and threw a startled glance back

over her shoulder, as if to see if anyone was watching them. Her fingers jerked in his clasp, but she did not pull away.

"Lord Morley, what . . .?" she began.

"Mrs. Chase—Rosalind," he said swiftly, aware that his time here with her was very short. "I am truly sorry about the wager, and about anything else I may have done to injure you. Please, I cannot be easy until I know you have forgiven me, or will at least *consider* forgiving me."

She stared down at their joined hands, staring at them as if there must be some answer written there in their linked fingers. "I—I will think about what you have said," she whispered. "Now I really must go."

"That is all I can ask for." Michael lifted her hand to his lips, and pressed a kiss to her fingertips. They trembled in his, like some wild, frightened bird. "Don't fly away from me," he begged.

He placed her hand carefully back in her lap, then leaped down from the phaeton and came around to help her alight. She backed away as soon as her feet touched the pavement, not looking into his eyes.

"Good afternoon, Lord Morley," she said, and hurried up the front steps to the door. All too soon, she had vanished behind the grand marble façade of Wayland House, more secure and distant than any vault.

But all was not lost, Michael vowed, as he climbed back up onto the phaeton. Not by a long distance. He had waited for too long to find Rosalind. He was not going to lose her now.

"So you are back!" Georgina called from beyond the half-open doors of the drawing room. "Come in and tell us about your drive in the park, Rosie."

Rosalind, her foot already on the first step of the staircase, cursed inwardly. She had so hoped to slip away from everyone, to escape into her chamber and nurse her headache—and her uncertainties—in solitude.

Now that was not to be. She would have to escape from Georgina first, which was no easy prospect.

Rosalind pasted a bright smile onto her face, and stepped past the drawing room doors. She did not go far beyond the threshold, though. That would just be inviting trouble, and she would never escape.

Georgina and Emily were playing a game of cards at a table by the window, while little Elizabeth Anne played nearby with her dolls. Georgina gave a smug little smile that Rosalind suspected had nothing to do with the hand of cards she held.

"How was your drive?" Georgina asked again. "Pleasant, I trust."

"Most pleasant," Rosalind replied in her most noncommittal tone. "The park was not yet overcrowded."

"And the weather most congenial, I am sure," Emily said. Her words were all that was innocent, but the smile that curved her lips was decidedly less so.

Rosalind feared Georgina's influence was rubbing off on the poor young lady. Rosalind thought she had best take her leave from the drawing room before it infected her, as well. She already felt enough like someone not herself.

"Yes," she said firmly. "The weather was very agreeable. But it *was* rather tiring to be out so long, so I think I will go to my chamber and rest before tea."

"An excellent notion," replied Georgina. "Alex procured tickets to the opera for us this evening, so you must keep up your strength. I do think that . . ." She paused, her eyes widening dramatically. "I just had a notion! Perhaps Lord Morley and his sister would care to join us."

"It is Mozart," Emily said. "*Idomeneo*. Most edifying."

Not Michael, not tonight! Rosalind thought in a near panic. Being in his presence made her feel so muddled, so unsure. Rather like drinking a bit too much champagne and feeling the room spin about, the floor tilt. It made her want to laugh, to dance.

She loved that feeling. And she hated it. She did

not yet know what to do with such new sensations.
Right now, she just wanted to lie down in her darkened room and try to figure out what to do with all
the things they had talked about today. Her own confessions, his silly wager, the feel of his kiss on her
hand . . . She could never sort all of that out if he
was next to her in a dim theater.

She could not show that to Georgina, though. It
would only urge her on in her mischief. "I think he
said he and Lady Violet already had an engagement,"
she said. She lied, of course; they had spoken of nothing so mundane.

"Oh, that is regrettable," said Georgina. "But we
will see him tomorrow evening at his father's soiree."

Oh, yes. Rosalind had forgotten about that for five
minutes. At least it was not until tomorrow. That
should give her some time to decide what to do next.
"I think I will just go upstairs now."

"Of course, Rosie dear. I will send up some tea.
You look rather pale."

Rosalind smiled at her, and turned to go. Before
she could make her escape, though, she heard Elizabeth Anne's little voice pipe up.

"Aunt Rosie," she called. "Are you going to marry
Lord Morley? You really should. He is *very*
handsome."

Georgina and Emily burst into laughter, and even
Rosalind could not entirely contain a smile. "No, Elizabeth Anne. I am not going to marry Lord Morley. I
am too old for him."

"Oh." Elizabeth Anne sounded very thoughtful.
"Well, then, perhaps I will marry him. I am not too
old for him."

"But you are too young, my darling," said Georgina, still laughing. "And I think your father will insist
on a prince for you, at the very least."

"Are there any princes as handsome as Lord Morley?" Elizabeth Anne asked.

Rosalind beat a hasty retreat before she could fall

onto the floor in mirth—and before she could think too deeply about Elizabeth Anne's questions of matrimony.

The little charmer was completely correct about one thing, though. Lord Morley was indeed very handsome.

Chapter Seventeen

"When hosting a soiree at your home, it is of utmost importance that you be certain your guests are comfortable at all times."
—*A Lady's Rules for Proper Behavior*, Chapter Four

"*A*re these flowers quite right here, Michael?" Violet asked anxiously, fussing with a vaseful of pink and white roses, moving them this way and that. They were only one of the many arrangements in the drawing room; Michael had never seen the gloomy expanse looking so cheerful. "Or would they appear to better advantage over there?"

Michael could not see any difference. "I think they are fine where they are."

"Fine? I want them to be *beautiful*." Violet's pretty face puckered in a concern far out of proportion to the dilemma.

Michael laughed, and reached out to tweak one of her curls. "They *are* beautiful. The room is lovely. You and Aunt Minnie have performed wonders here."

Violet finally smiled, a rueful little grin. She left off shifting the flowers around and pushed her curls back from her forehead. "I am being silly, I know. But this is the first time I have been allowed to attend a *real* London party."

"And the first party that has been held here since Mother died," Michael said. "I understand that you are nervous, Vi, but I promise you that all will be well. It isn't a grand ball or anything of that sort."

"No. I think I would faint if it was! I asked Mrs. Chase to come a bit early. I will not be so nervous if she is here."

Mrs. Chase. Michael's breath caught at the merest mention of her name. He had not heard from her at all since their drive yesterday, though he had sent her the biggest bouquet of red roses he could find this morning. *Would* she come early? Or had she run as far as she could from him and his wild ways and his impossible family? He could scarcely blame her if she had.

But he deeply, desperately hoped that she had not.

He had no idea where their strange new friendship, so delicate and odd and lovely, was going. Or if it was going anywhere at all. He only knew that he wanted to, he *had* to, see her again.

"Michael?" Violet asked. "Are you quite all right? You looked so strange all of a sudden."

He made himself smile at her reassuringly. "I am quite well, Vi. You said Mrs. Chase is coming early?"

"I do hope so. I sent her a note only this afternoon."

"Violet, dearest! You are not even dressed yet," Aunt Minnie cried as she bustled into the drawing room, tweaking a flower here and there, straightening a chair and some objets d'art. "Go upstairs at once, child."

"But I need to see if . . ." Violet began.

"Do not argue, young lady! Go and change your gown. Guests will be arriving soon."

"Very well, Aunt Minnie." Violet gave Michael one last harried smile, and hurried away.

Aunt Minnie laughed. "That girl needs to move in Society more!"

"She will make her bow next year. That will be soon enough."

"Indeed. She ought to become accustomed to being a hostess sooner than that, though."

"I am sure she will. She is learning a great many of the social arts at her school."

"Ah, yes. With the excellent Mrs. Chase. I understand she will be here tonight."

Here. She would be here, in only an hour or two. "Yes."

"I look forward to meeting her. I have heard that she has been seen quite often in your company of late, my dear." Aunt Minnie gave him a shrewd glance. "You know, Michael, I have attended many evenings such as this—more than I would care to count. But I have a strange feeling about tonight."

Michael felt a chill in his fingertips, a tingle of some strange foreboding. "A feeling, Aunt Minnie?"

She laughed, and waved her hand in a careless, dismissive little gesture. "Oh, I am just a silly old woman! Still, I think something *will* happen tonight. Perhaps something good? We can only hope."

Rosalind stared up at Bronston House as they stepped down from the carriage and climbed the shallow, stone front steps. It was certainly not a structure that could be called charming or fashionable. It was too dark, too foreboding, too—too *looming*. Even the golden light that glowed from its windows for the party failed to add much warmth to the chilly aspect. Rosalind shivered a bit as she took it all in.

After they handed their wraps to the footman in the foyer, Georgina took Rosalind's arm as they made their way into the drawing room. "Such a musty old pile!" she whispered. "And just look at those draperies. Thirty years out of date at least. But I do think it has potential. The lines are good, and the carvings on that panel very fine. The right woman could really make something of it."

The right woman? A woman such as Rosalind herself, mayhap? Rosalind almost laughed at such obvious machinations. If only Georgina would not say such things *here*, where anyone might overhear her! "Georgina . . ." she said warningly.

"Oh, pish! I am not saying anything untoward, Rosie. I merely mentioned that a woman of taste, with the Bronston money, could really transform this place. Beginning with taking away that awful table. Elephant legs! How perfectly horrid."

Rosalind had to agree about the table. That was certainly a horror of the first order. Yet she was not likely to be the one who cleared away the clutter, or did anything at all with this mausoleum of a house. Fortunately, there was no time to speak of this further. They had reached the drawing room, and Lady Violet was waiting to greet them.

"Mrs. Chase!" the girl said happily. "I am so glad you decided to attend our little gathering. What a beautiful gown."

Rosalind was wearing borrowed plumes again, a dark blue silk trimmed with silver beadwork and ribbons that Georgina had insisted she had ordered and then hated, so of course the gown was beautiful. It was Lady Violet who truly appeared lovely, though, in a white muslin gown edged in purple satin ribbons and trimmed with artificial violets. "And you look most charming, Lady Violet. Such a grown-up young lady."

Violet gave her a wide, pleased smile, then closed her eyes for an instant, as if steeling herself for a task. "You have not yet greeted my father, Mrs. Chase. Father, of course you remember Mrs. Chase. Mrs. Chase, the Earl of Athley."

Rosalind turned to face the earl. She had indeed only met him briefly once or twice, but she knew very well that Violet held not much fondness for him, and Michael had dropped hints that all was not well in Bronston House. Now she could see why the free-spirited Michael and the gentle Violet might be less than cozy with their father.

The earl did not rise from his chair. Indeed, he hardly acknowledged them at all. His feet appeared so swollen with gout that to stand would have been a very difficult undertaking, and it was clear that he felt

a mere schoolmistress did not warrant such effort. He
gave her a small nod, and no smile of greeting pierced
the gloom of his wrinkled, sour, yellow-tinged visage.
"Yes. You own that Seminary for Young Ladies," he
said. He brightened a bit when he turned to Georgina,
though. She, after all, was a duchess, even if she was
also an artist.

As Georgina made her pleasantries to the earl, Rosalind stepped farther into the room and surveyed the
gathered guests. It was not a large crowd; this was just
a quiet evening of supper and cards for a young lady
not yet out. But there were certainly a great many
people, of a wide variety of ages, from the ancient
Lady Day-Hamilton with her ear trumpet to the
youthful Mr. Gilmore and Lord Carteret. When Rosalind saw them, lounging indolently over by the marble
fireplace, she gave a prayer of thanksgiving that Allen
was far away from them right now. It gave her one
less thing to worry about.

Her main worry was walking toward her right now.
And he looked more dangerously handsome than
ever, with a claret-colored velvet coat fit perfectly over
his strong shoulders and a pale pink cravat wrapped
about his tanned throat. One ink-dark curl fell carelessly over his brow, and Rosalind's fingers almost
itched to push it back, to feel that rough satin.

She was reminded all too clearly of their kiss on
that moonlit terrace. Her gaze flickered involuntarily
to the drawing room windows, but she saw no terrace
beyond. Only night.

"Mrs. Chase," he said, and raised her hand to his
lips for a salute that lingered just a bit longer than the
rules specified. "How delightful to see you again. It
has been far too long."

Rosalind couldn't help but smile. He almost always
had that effect on her—if she did not fight against it.
Fighting against his charm was futile, anyway, as she
always found when she was in his presence. She was
being drawn in by it now. Everything, everyone else
in the drawing room faded away.

Oh, I am in trouble, she thought as she took her hand back. "Too long, Lord Morley? We were in the park just yesterday afternoon."

"An eternity ago. I am happy you came here this evening; I fear this soiree would be too dull without you."

"Dull?" She glanced about, searching for something positive to comment on. It was a quiet gathering, despite the varied guests, and the room did not much improve on closer acquaintance. The furniture was old, dark, and heavy, barely disguised by candleglow and copious arrangements of pink and white flowers. A carved stone family crest of spectacular ugliness hung above the fireplace.

"Your home is—very cozy," she managed to say. "Most singular."

"A moldy cave, you mean," he answered cheerfully. "Thankfully, it is not yet *my* house. I only have to visit it on occasion. But come, Mrs. Chase, let me introduce you to my aunt, Lady Minerva Fielding. She is most eager to greet you."

"Is she, indeed?" Rosalind wondered why Lady Minerva would be eager to greet *her,* and she felt a quick bolt of panic. But she had already realized that she would have to give up her usual iron control this evening. "Then I would be very pleased to meet her."

Michael held his arm out to her, and she slid her hand into the crook of his elbow. It was all very proper, yet somehow *felt* thrilling and dangerous. That was part of his power, she realized. He could make the everyday seem extraordinary.

"And I hope you will allow me to escort you in to supper later?" he asked.

"Supper?" She drew back to peer up at him. "Surely there are ladies here of far higher rank to whom you should give that honor."

He leaned closer and murmured warmly into her ear, "*You* are the most important lady I see, Rosalind. Here, or anywhere else. Please—come in to supper with me."

Rosalind could only nod; no words could press their way past the knot in her throat. No one had ever said such things to her before, and she had always thought herself immune to sweet words and flattery. She was too old, too sensible for such things.

Apparently, she had been wrong, very wrong indeed, for she felt flushed from head to toe with a strange, charmed pleasure. Her blushes probably clashed horribly with her hair, but she could not seem to care.

"Very well," she whispered. "I would be happy to go in to supper with you—Michael."

Michael. Michael. He still heard his name spoken in her soft, rough whisper, even as they sat down to supper. The conversation that swirled around him had no meaning, no coherence. The food that was placed before him seemed tasteless, bland, even though Aunt Minnie had brought in a fine caterer for the evening. Rosalind had spoken his name, had looked at him with a wide-eyed surprise that made her seem so very young and vulnerable, so very dear.

How had he not seen this the very first time he ever laid eyes on her? How had he ever thought her a humorless, rule-following matron? She might have written the rules, but now she was surely coming to see things his way. She had already gone so far as to kiss him. She just needed one small push—right into his arms.

There were such fires beneath her chill façade. He could see even now that she was struggling between following her old, safe path, and letting herself fly free. She kept giving him quick, darting glances from the corner of her eye. Her fingers were tight on the heavy silver handle of her fork, and she lifted her wineglass to her lips more often than she was surely accustomed to. She laughed freely at the admittedly weak jokes of the man at her other side. These were all very good signs that she was beginning to enjoy her life anew.

Then he noticed, tucked into the vibrant red curls

that were swept atop her head, one scarlet rosebud
fastened with a sapphire clip. A rosebud from the bouquet he sent her after their drive.

Yes, he thought, trying not to be too smug. One
tiny push, and a lady and her rules would be parted.
Under the tablecloth, he gently, surreptitiously,
pressed his leg against hers through her skirt.

She jerked and stiffened—but she did not move
away. She just took another sip of wine, and gave him
a small smile.

"My brother is soon to have another volume of poetry published," Violet said, breaking into his pleasant
ruminations. "He is becoming so well-known. As great
as Byron."

He left off gazing at Rosalind to smile at his sister.
"My verses are not nearly as great as Byron's, Violet."

"It is a sister's prerogative to brag about her brother,
and so I shall," Violet said stoutly. "They *are* great
poems, and I am sure everyone here would agree."

A murmur of laughter and assent rose around the
table, and the conversation turned generally to poetry
and literature. The lady on Michael's other side asked
him a question about the new volume, and he turned
to answer her. Yet he was still very aware of Rosalind's warmth next to him, her fresh, soft scent. Once,
she even smiled at him.

Things were all going extraordinarily well, for an
evening he had so dreaded. But then his father, so
uncharacteristically quiet and subdued throughout
supper, finished his fourth glass of wine and tapped
the edge of the crystal for a fifth.

"Demmed ridiculous way for a man to pass his time,
spouting poetry," he announced querulously. Aunt
Minnie tried to put her hand on his arm, to rein him
in, but he shook her off. "A shame he is the only heir
I have, but his mother was a bloodless woman. She
had no bottom, gave out after two mewling babes.
And now my daughter is the same! Inviting curates
and schoolmistresses into the house. What is Society
coming to? I ask you!"

He left off on a groan. Aunt Minnie had apparently just given him a quick kick to his gouty leg beneath the table. The earl subsided to quiet mutters into his wineglass.

Michael felt a rush of fury, a white-hot tide that was too familiar whenever he was in the presence of his father. The earl had never been renowned for his sparkling good behavior, but this was the outside of enough. Violet had so looked forward to this evening, and now she appeared pale and stricken.

Rosalind drew away from Michael, and would not meet his gaze. Across the table, the Duchess of Wayland watched her friend with a concerned frown.

Michael wanted more than anything to leap across the table and strangle his father, yet he knew he could not. He would not make the evening any more difficult for the women he cared about.

"My father is also writing a book," he said loudly. "On the great downfall of civilization. His theory is that art and civility are killing us. This evening, with such congenial company and fine cuisine, is hastening its demise. I say we finally send it on its way *after* cards."

There was a wave of relieved laughter, and conversation resumed its steady hum. Violet's rosy color returned to her cheeks, and she smiled at the young man—the curate—seated to her left.

Yet Rosalind still would not look at him.

Rosalind studied the array of cards in her hand, unable to fully comprehend the numbers and suits. Usually she quite enjoyed a pleasant game of piquet, but tonight it was a struggle. She had to rely on Georgina's promptings to carry her through.

She peered over the top of the cards to see the dark corner where the old earl sat slumped in sleep. He was truly horrid, just as Violet and Michael had hinted. It was a very good thing that he almost never went into Society. He could have very much benefited from a copy of her *Rules*.

Yet the old curmudgeon had been right about one thing. A schoolmistress had no place here. She should probably be grateful to the man for stopping her now, before she made an even greater fool of herself than she already had. She ought to go back to her school, before London began to gossip about the ridiculous schoolmistress widow who chased after the young poet viscount. She should cease playing dress-up in Georgina's gowns and go back to her real life.

She had not yet achieved all her objectives in Town. There were still Allen's debts. Yet she thought that now Michael—Lord Morley—would not go on trying to undermine her *Rules*. Not now that they knew each other, not now that they were—well, friends of a sort. Perhaps she could rebuild that book's popularity, finish her second edition, and go forward.

Somehow, though, that thought did not fill her with the elation it once would have.

"Mrs. Chase?" her piquet partner said, bringing her back to the reality of the moment. "It is your trick."

Rosalind gave him an apologetic smile, and collected her cards. As her partner laid down new cards, she examined the players gathered at other tables. Michael played with Lady Emily, and gave Rosalind a grin when he met her gaze. She turned away before the temptation to grin in return overtook her.

Lady Violet did not play cards, but she sat beside one of the open windows with her aunt and two other people. Of Allen's troublemaking friends, Gilmore and Carteret, there was no sign. She had actually not seen them since supper.

She sincerely hoped that meant they had gone home, and would thus do nothing to spoil the rest of this evening. Poor Lady Violet had enough to contend with in her own father.

"I am not sure this is such a good idea," Gilmore said, glancing nervously over his shoulder to see if anyone was watching. He and Carteret had slipped back into the dining room when everyone was occupied at the card tables. The supper remains had been cleared away, and tea and cakes were laid out for after the games were ended. The centerpiece was a large crystal punch bowl, filled with a weak claret cup.

"Nonsense, Gilmore! Don't be so very chicken-hearted. No one is watching, they are all too occupied with dull old cards. I vow, this is the most boring event I have attended all Season. I never would have come if my father had not insisted. This will just liven things up a bit, and no harm done." Carteret reached inside his coat and pulled out a silver flask. As he uncorked it, the pungent fumes of strongest Scotch whiskey floated out into the room.

"But I think you should . . ." Gilmore began to protest again. It did no good, for Carteret proceeded to pour the entire contents into the punch bowl.

The amber-colored liquid disappeared into the insipid pink punch. Carteret picked up a crystal ladle and stirred it in.

"They will thank us for giving them a bit of amusement," Carteret said, with a smirk. "And someone has to fight stuffy propriety, since it seems Lord Morley will not. Only a few weeks ago he was insisting no one had to follow the rules, and now he is the very pattern card of propriety! He is even dancing attendance on Lucas's sister. This will surely help him to recover."

Carteret laughed, and Gilmore did not like the sound of that chuckle at all. It was not a sound of mirth and mischief, but hollow and humorless. Yet there was nothing he could do now. The murmur of voices and laughter was approaching the dining room, and Carteret and Gilmore stepped back away from the table. Lady Violet and her aunt came into the room and went to examine the refreshments.

Gilmore could say nothing now without exposing his own role in the prank.

Violet did not feel well at all.

The room was spinning around her head in a most

odd way, and she was uncomfortably warm even when she discarded her shawl. Her temples throbbed, and everything was blurry at the edges. She turned and blinked at her brother, who stood several feet away conversing with Mrs. Chase and the Duchess of Wayland. His image wavered, and she turned away.

Perhaps some more of that punch would help. It was cool at least. She made her way unsteadily to the bowl and ladled the pink liquid into her glass. It sloshed over the sides as her hand trembled, but some of it made its way into the receptacle. She sipped at it, then gulped greedily. Really, it tasted much better than claret cup ever had before!

Violet giggled, and bumped into a chair. Where had that come from? She stumbled over the gilt frame, giggling even louder. She could not seem to *stop* laughing, even though there was really nothing funny.

"This is all very odd. I must be quite ill indeed," she whispered, and hiccuped.

A hand touched her arm gently, and she spun around. The room tilted crazily, and she would have fallen if the touch had not tightened. She blinked up at—Lord Carteret.

How odd, she thought dimly. She had met Lord Carteret once or twice before—he belonged to the same club as her brother. Yet she had never before noticed that he was really quite good-looking.

She gave him a smile, and giggled again.

"Lady Violet, are you well?" he asked. She thought he also smiled, but really she must have been mistaken, for when she blinked and looked again there was only concern on his face.

"I—I am not really sure," she answered. She pressed her hand to her head, hoping that would stop the incessant spinning.

"Come, let me take you outside for some fresh air. It will help you feel better in no time." He took her arm in his secure clasp and led her toward the doors leading out to the garden.

"I—well—" Violet murmured uncertainly. Surely it

was against the rules to go outside alone with a gentleman? Yet no one seemed to notice at all. They were all laughing, and talking very loudly. Too loudly. It made her headache worse.

Surely if no one was noticing, it was quite all right. And she did long for a breath of fresh air. She was just so *warm*.

"Thank you, Lord Carteret," she said, leaning on his arm. "I would like some air."

"Not at all, Lady Violet," he answered solicitously. "I am only concerned for your comfort."

"Michael, my dear, have you seen Violet?"

Michael turned from his conversation with Rosalind and the duchess to see his aunt hurrying toward him, a concerned expression on her face.

A cold frisson danced along his spine, which was thoroughly ridiculous, of course. What could happen to Violet in her own home? There were dozens of people about. He glanced quickly around the room, at the guests who sipped at tea and punch, milled aimlessly, chatted. His father sat over in a corner, as sour as ever despite the obsequious people who gathered about him.

Violet was not among any of the groups.

"I have not seen her, Aunt Minnie," he said, taking her arm. "But I am sure she cannot be far. Perhaps a servant came to her with some sort of refreshment emergency?"

Aunt Minnie nodded, the feathers on her turban bobbing, but she still appeared far from certain. "Perhaps. She usually tells me before she leaves. She is not the *boldest* of girls, you know. It is not like her to just run away like that."

Michael *did* know what his sister was like—terrified of appearing rude or breaking a rule. That chill instinct increased. "I will go and find her, Aunt Minnie."

"And I will help you," Rosalind said. She turned away to put her empty cup down on a table, and brushed her hands together briskly. "Surely with two of us searching, she will be found in a trice. She could not have gone far."

Michael *wanted* to have her with him. His Rosalind had an air of such efficiency that he was sure she would find any errant girl right off. And if Violet was, heaven forbid, in some sort of trouble, it would be good to have a woman with her.

But if they somehow found themselves alone in a dark corridor, or a shadowed garden . . .

He thought of their kiss on that terrace. He remembered the feel of her in his arms, the taste of her light breath on his lips, and he almost groaned aloud.

You are looking for your sister, man, he told himself sternly. *Don't forget that.*

There would be time for plotting seductions later, after Violet was safely found. And after he discovered whether or not Rosalind had forgiven him for his boyish wager. For all he knew, she might never let him set a finger on her again.

"Thank you, Mrs. Chase," he said. "I would be very glad of your assistance."

"I will fetch my husband to help me search the garden," the duchess said, already turning away. "Lady Violet probably wanted a breath of fresh air. It has suddenly become rather—raucous in here."

Rosalind slid her hand over his sleeve lightly as they left the dining room and headed for the deserted portion of the house. At least now he knew that she *would* touch him, even if in such a formal way.

If only he knew where his sister was, as well. And why it was suddenly so very loud in the dining room.

"Where are we, Lord Carteret?" Violet murmured. Her dizziness had only increased since they left the dining room, and a bright light flashed in her head even though the room was dim. She rubbed her hand over her eyes, and saw that they were in the seldom-used conservatory.

Her brother had once told her that their mother had loved the conservatory, had lavished care on the plants and flowers. Now it was neglected, overgrown with tangles of brown and green vines, littered with empty clay pots. Moonlight beamed down from the glass panels overhead, turning the whole place into a shifting, crawling, *living* thing.

Violet felt queasy, and so very warm. She stripped off her long kid gloves and dropped them onto the floor before stumbling across the room to collapse in a wrought iron chaise. The cushions were long gone, but she did not care. She just wanted to sit down. It was so very *warm* . . .

Lord Carteret sat down next to her and took her hand, startling her. She had quite forgotten he was there, and was utterly bewildered when he pressed his lips to her bare fingers.

"What are you doing?" she gasped, and tried to pull away from him.

His clasp tightened, and his other arm came around her shoulders. "Shh, Lady Violet," he said thickly. "You've been dying for my kisses since the moment we met. All the ladies do." He pushed her back so that the iron lattice pattern of the chaise bit through her thin muslin dress into her skin.

"Let me go!" she cried, and tried to shove him away. But he was too strong, and she was too dizzyingly bewildered. This all seemed too unreal, like a terrible dream she could not wake herself from.

"You are so beautiful," he muttered hoarsely. "Why have I never seen it before? Kiss me, Lady Violet!"

"No!" Violet turned her face away frantically, and his wet lips landed on her neck. His hand slid down her arm, pushing her short sleeve off her shoulder. "This is against the rules!"

Rosalind did not like this house. She knew that this was the family house of two people she cared about, Michael and Lady Violet, but she still could not like it. She was not a woman who believed in malevolent spirits, or any spirits at all for that matter, yet if she did she would say they dwelled here. The carpets and furniture were dark and heavy, adding to the gloom and the airlessness. A chill seemed to emanate from the very walls.

She shivered.

Michael glanced down at her. "Is something amiss?"

She peered up at him. His beauty was like a beacon in this gloomy place. After meeting his father and seeing this place, she marveled at his humor and kindness, at his sister's sweetness.

He appeared so like an angel now, watching over her, protecting her from this darkness. She had ceased utterly to care about the color of his neckcloths or all the rules he broke when he went about in Society. She could not even care any longer that he was a viscount, that he was younger than she, that he wrote poetry and she was dull and prosaic.

Here, in this instant, she did not care about those things at all.

"I am fine," she answered. "Or I will be when we find Lady Violet."

Michael nodded, and his angel's face darkened with worry. "Surely she could not have gone far."

Rosalind glanced about again. She half-suspected that Violet could have been snatched away by evil fairies in such a place as this, but of course that was nonsense. Violet had to be *somewhere*. "We checked the library and the morning room. Her maid is checking in her chamber. Where else is there?"

Michael frowned, and shook his head. "This is not a vast house. I think we have looked everywhere . . ." His brow cleared. "Of course! The conservatory."

"The conservatory?"

"It was my mother's favorite place. People seldom go there now. Perhaps Violet went there to find some air without going outside to the gardens."

He led her to the end of the corridor and they turned off onto a flagstone walkway illuminated by skylights overhead. At the end could be seen double doors made of glass, standing open. Rosalind stumbled

a bit on the uneven stones, and as Michael steadied
her with an arm about her waist, they heard a scream.

"No! This is against the rules!"

There was a great crash—and Rosalind and Michael
broke into a run.

Chapter Eighteen

"A true gentleman shall never press his attentions on a lady—if this happens, he is not a gentleman, and the lady should disentangle herself from the situation by whatever means necessary."
—*A Lady's Rules for Proper Behavior,* Chapter Thirteen

*R*osalind pulled away from Michael and ran the last few steps into the conservatory, with him close on her heels. She burst through the doors—and froze at the scene that greeted her.

Violet stood huddled against a long plant stand, her pale curls disheveled and one short, puffed sleeve falling from her shoulder. One trembling hand was pressed to her lips; the other held the shattered rim of a clay pot.

Rosalind heard a low moan, and her gaze swung from Violet to the man collapsed on the stone floor. Shards of the pot were scattered around him, with dirt and dried leaves dusting his hair and his elegant coat. He blinked, trying to focus, as he slowly sat up, one hand holding his head. She saw that it was Lord Carteret.

A red-hot anger bloomed in her heart, deeper than any she had ever known, or even imagined, before. This—this *cad* had taken advantage of Violet, sweet Violet! She lurched one blind step in his direction, intending to scratch out his eyes with her bare nails, but she was stopped by a choked sob from Violet.

Rosalind swung away from Lord Carteret, and stepped over his legs, lifting her hem as if he was a piece of sewer flotsam that could soil the fine blue silk. She hurried over to Violet and anchored her arms about the girl's trembling shoulders.

Violet dropped the remains of the pot and collapsed against Rosalind. "How could he do that?" she cried. "It was against the rules, Mrs. Chase! It was against the rules."

"Shh, my dear. You are safe now, don't cry." Rosalind patted Violet's back as if she were a frightened infant, and pressed her cheek lightly against the girl's hair.

She drew in a deep breath—and paused, frowning. She could smell Violet's perfume, a light violet and rosebud scent, but there was something underneath. Something sharp and sour.

"Violet, my dear," she said softly, careful not to raise her voice and alarm the girl. "What have you been drinking this evening?"

"Drinking?" Violet drew back to peer up at Rosalind, her face creased in confusion. "Only tea, and wine with dinner. Oh, and some punch."

"Punch?" Rosalind then saw the crystal punch glass, half rolled under an iron chaise.

"Yes. The claret cup."

That was *not* claret Rosalind smelled. It was strong whiskey, of the sort her husband had indulged in on rare occasions. She gently propped Violet back against the plant stand, as if she was a wax doll, and bent down to retrieve the glass. Most of the contents had been drunk or spilled out, but there were still a few dregs in the very bottom. Rosalind sniffed cautiously.

Yes. Most definitely whiskey.

She looked up, searching for Michael. She had almost forgotten he had raced behind her into the room, in all the excitement of her temper and comforting

Violet. She could not forget him now, though. He had his fists around the lapels of Carteret's coat and was roughly hauling the groggy young man to his feet. On Michael's face she saw written the utter fury she herself had felt so deeply. His sensual lips were thinned to an angry line, his jaw tight.

And a new fear took hold in her heart—the fear that Michael might fight, even challenge Carteret to a duel. As much as she wanted to see Carteret punished for his dastardly deed tonight, she could not bear to see Michael hurt. She could not see *two* people she cared about in pain this eve.

"Michael," she called sharply. "Could you come over here for a moment, please?"

He glanced toward her, frowning as if puzzled that she was there. His hands were still tight on Carteret, who was moaning and brushing feebly at Michael with ineffectual motions. Rosalind held the glass up.

Michael pushed Carteret back to the floor and came to her side, still keeping a sharp eye on the prone young man. "What is it, Rosie?" he said roughly, impatiently.

"I think Violet has been drinking strong spirits," Rosalind whispered. "There was whiskey in this glass, and she seems terribly disoriented."

"My sister has never had anything stronger than watered wine in her life!" he protested vehemently.

"I am not suggesting that Violet became foxed on purpose. She is not a girl to make such mischief. I am merely suggesting that she is in a very poor condition right now, and I ought to escort her upstairs."

"That is a very good idea. I don't want Violet here while I deal with that—that—"

He uttered a word that was most assuredly against the rules, yet Rosalind could not chide him. It expressed her own sentiments toward Carteret exactly. But she did not at all like the darkness shadowing Michael's beautiful eyes. She caught his hand between both of hers and held him beside her.

"Promise me that you will not do something like challenge Lord Carteret to a duel."

"Rosie," he answered, curling his fingers around hers. "He plied my sister with whiskey, and lured her in here to take advantage of her! How can I let these things go unchallenged?"

"They need not go unchallenged. I am sure he will pay—he is paying already." She gestured toward Lord Carteret, who still lay in a heap on the floor, moaning about his aching head. "Violet took care of herself with him, but she cannot take care of herself all the time. She needs you here, in her life, to help her. Not dead in some field, shot through the head."

"I would not be the one lying there. I am an excellent shot, Rosie."

"But what if Lord Carteret cheated? If he does not scruple at giving young ladies strong drink, he would not at turning before the count of ten." She leaned closer to him, clinging to his hand. She could not remember ever feeling more *desperate* before in her life. "Please, Michael. Violet needs you. *I* need you. Promise me that, whatever you do, you will not fight."

His expression eased a bit, the sharp crease between his eyes softening as he stared down at her. "Very well. For you, I will not fight."

Rosalind nodded, her heart lightened even if only a small bit. "Very good. I will hold you to that. And now I must take Violet upstairs before she becomes ill."

"Of course." Michael kissed her cheek quickly and released her hands. "What did Vi and I ever do before you came into our lives, Rosie? You are an angel."

An angel. Funny—that was exactly what she had thought about *him*. Smiling secretly, she went to Violet and wrapped her arm around the girl. "Come, my dear, let me take you up to your chamber. You will feel better after you have washed your face and lain down on your bed for a few moments."

Violet nodded weakly, and released her death grip

on the plant stand. She did look rather green, but at least her eyes were no longer glazed and clouded with shock. "Yes," she murmured. "I feel a bit queasy, Mrs. Chase."

"I will send for some strong tea. That will settle your stomach."

Violet leaned against her. "People are probably talking about me. Saying dreadful things."

"Not at all. No one even knows you left the party except for me, your brother, your aunt, and the Waylands. We would never tell a soul; we are concerned only for your safety."

Tears trickled down Violet's flushed cheeks, silent harbingers of misery. "I was so stupid, Mrs. Chase! So very stupid."

"Not at all, my dear. This was not your fault at all. It was entirely Lord Carteret's. He is a very bad man."

"He broke the rules!" Violet cried. "So very many rules."

Violet's words reverberated in Michael's mind long after Rosalind had led her from the conservatory. *The rules.* Carteret had broken the rules. Violet seemed quite obsessed on that point.

Michael turned to stare down at Carteret where he huddled on the floor. The man—or boy, really, as he could hardly be older than eighteen—appeared crumpled and miserable on the flagstones. But when he peered up at Michael, his bleary eyes burned with a strange resentment, a glowing, sullen fire.

For the first time, Michael had some idea of what had driven Rosalind to write those rules. It was not from some manic compulsion to control the behavior of others, as he had once imagined, before he knew her. It was to impose some order, some limits to the actions of people like Carteret. People who would take advantage of innocents like Violet—such as Rosalind had surely once been.

Women were weak, not only physically but within the dictates of Society. He had always known this, of course; it was self-evident, a part of everyday life. But he had never really *known* that, not until this moment. Rosalind had devised those rules to give the girls at her school some power over what happened to them. If all of Society insisted on following the rules, even men like Carteret and his ilk would have to fall into line or be ostracized. They were a flimsy protection at best, yet somehow Rosalind had managed to make it strong—until he came along and undermined both her and her rules.

Mindless obedience to dictates would *never* be right in his mind. But some rules were necessary, and he had been an utter fool not to see that before. He owed Rosalind a great apology.

He strode up to Carteret and nudged him with the toe of his shoe. "Get up," Michael ordered brusquely. "And cease moaning."

"Your chit of a sister nearly broke my head," Carteret whined. He held his hand away from his wound to show Michael the blood there.

"You deserved far worse. I said get up."

Carteret used the frame of the iron chaise to haul himself upright. He really did look to be in bad shape, with blood dripping from the cut on his head and his coat sleeve torn. Michael mentally applauded his sister for attempting to take her pound of flesh.

Carteret sneered at him, or at least tried to. It came out looking more like a pout. "Are you going to call me out? Demand that I name my seconds?"

"Sorry to disappoint you, but not tonight."

Carteret's sneer dissolved into surprise. "N—no?"

"No. But if anything of this sort ever happens again, I will not so restrain myself. For tonight, it is sufficient that you remove yourself and your friend Mr. Gilmore from my family's house. In future, you will never show your face at the Thoth Club again."

"No!" Carteret cried out. "Not the club! I must have . . ."

"You will *not* be a member of the club any longer. Your name will be stricken from the rolls. And you will never contact, speak to, or look at my sister, Mrs. Chase, or Mr. Lucas. Is that perfectly clear?"

Carteret gave him a sullen nod. He could clearly see that Michael meant every word he said, and would never be swayed by pleas or threats. Carteret's days at the Thoth Club were finished.

"Excellent. Now leave, before you bleed any further onto the floor."

With one last glare, Carteret hurried out of the room, his footsteps fading away down the corridor. Michael had the suspicious feeling that he had not heard the last of that young man, but for now he was gone. It was all echoing silence in the conservatory.

Michael straightened his coat and cravat, and ran his fingers through his disheveled hair. He filled his lungs with the cool evening air that flowed from the open windows and slowly released a breath, trying to let go of his raw anger.

Once he felt as if he could face the civilized world again without disgracing himself, he followed Carteret's path down the corridor. He had to make sure the cad left, and then he would send Aunt Minnie up to Violet's chamber, and tell the Duchess of Wayland that their quarry had been safely found.

And then—then he knew exactly what he had to do.

Rosalind slowly made her way down the staircase back toward the party. She had left Violet, still queasy and teary but much calmed, to the capable ministrations of her aunt. She had taken Violet's hairbrush to her own mussed curls and smoothed her gown. Now there was nothing to do but rejoin the fray.

She wondered, feared, what she would find there. Would Michael be off with his seconds, going to fight Lord Carteret with pistols at dawn? Or would he keep his word to her?

She knew that, under ordinary circumstances, Michael would always keep his promises. But she had never seen him look as he had this night, when faced with Carteret's villainy. Michael was usually so very affable, so full of jests and easy good humor. He could always make her smile or laugh, as no one else ever had before. Tonight, he had looked like a stranger, with a killing fire behind his eyes.

In that moment, she knew he was capable of a duel, but she prayed a challenge had not gone forth. If he killed Carteret, he would be forced to flee. And if he was killed himself . . .

Rosalind's breath caught on a sob. She pressed her hand to her throat. Neither of those things would happen. He had promised her.

She forced her breath past the lump in her throat and stepped into the drawing room. It was very clear from just one glance that Violet had not been the only one to unwittingly imbibe this evening. Laughter and conversation were loud, even deafening. The earl was asleep on one of the settees, snoring loudly. An impromptu game of boules was being played from one end of the marble floor to the other. Someone banged out a wild waltz on a dreadfully out of tune pianoforte while couples whirled about unsteadily.

This was like a scene from Dante, one of the tiers of hell—proper London Society gone mad, flying high on whiskey. It was almost as if the people had never had a drink before in their lives.

Rosalind laughed helplessly. So many rules were being broken she could not even count them! Yet she did not care. She just wanted to find Michael.

Ordinarily, she was sure he would be right in the thick of things, playing boules with the others. He was not there, nor at the pianoforte. He was not anywhere in the room.

"Rosalind!" she heard a voice call. Rosalind turned to see Georgina hurrying toward her through the crowd. "Lord Morley told us that Lady Violet was found. I trust that she is well?"

"Yes, she is fine. Or soon will be. Lady Minerva is with her now. But have you seen Lord Morley recently? Do you know where he has gone?"

Georgina gave her a knowing little smile. "Oh, yes. He wants you to meet him in the garden."

"The garden?"

"Yes. By the Cupid fountain, he said."

Oh, thank heaven, Rosalind thought. So he had not gone to duel. He was waiting for her in the garden. She hurried out of the drawing room to the doors leading into the night-darkened garden.

She was so relieved she did not even stop to think about the oddness of the invitation, or of Georgina's smug smile that was always a portent of mischief. She just wanted to see Michael.

The garden was very dark and quiet, the gravel pathways lit only by the moon and the clear stars. It was obvious that the earl cared little about horticulture; the flower beds were sparse, the borders overgrown. But there were many marble benches and statues of classical figures along the way. They shone with an opalescent glow, lighting her way to the center of the garden where the Cupid fountain waited. The music of water burbled and flowed, drowning out the remnants of voices from the open windows at the party.

The Cupid waited—but not Michael.

Rosalind spun about in a circle. She could not see him anywhere, not even at the shadowed edges of the pathway. Her slippers ground on the gravel as she strolled to the fountain. A cool wind flowed over her, and she shivered. She had been in such a hurry she left the house without her shawl.

Her stomach still fluttered with excitement, anticipation. She had never met a man in a dark garden, not even when she was young and Charles was courting her. It was such a small thing, really, especially compared with all the things she had done in the last few days. But it *felt* daring. It felt wicked. And so very delicious.

If only he was here. She began to fear that perhaps he had gone off to fight after all.

She perched on the edge of the fountain, the hard marble cold beneath the thin silk of her gown. As she wrapped her arms over her waist, a whisper came to her on the breeze.

"Rosie," it said. "Psst! Rosie!"

Rosalind shot up from her seat, glancing about frantically. "Michael! Where are you?"

"Up here."

"Up—where?" She peered up into the sky, perplexed.

"*Here*. In the tree."

She whirled around—and finally saw him. He sat on one of the thick, lower-hanging branches of a stout oak tree. His back was braced on the trunk, his legs dangling down.

"Good evening," he said, grinning at her.

Rosalind choked on a laugh. "You ridiculous man! Whatever are you doing up there?"

"Waiting for you, of course." He leaned down and held his hand out to her, beckoning with his fingers. "Come up and join me?"

Climb a tree? Rosalind inched a step back. There was probably not a rule against it, per se, but it could not be proper. And her skirts were far too cumbersome.

It was impossible. Really. Truly.

Wasn't it?

"Come on," he coaxed, in a low, tempting voice. "It is very pleasant up here. Very—private."

"My skirts . . ."

"This isn't up very high. You won't even have to climb, I'll help you up."

Rosalind glanced back over her shoulder. There was no one in the garden. They were all alone in the dark.

"Come on, Rosie," he said. "It is easy."

Rosalind took one step closer, then another, and another. She reached up and clasped his hand.

"Didn't Eve get into trouble in just such a garden?" she murmured.

"But I am so much better-looking than an old serpent," he said with a laugh.

"And not a bit conceited about it, either," she answered tartly.

"Of course not. I am modesty personified."

"Certainly. Now, how do you propose I get myself up there?"

"Do you see that large knot in the wood there? Give me your other hand and then put your foot on it. On the count of three, push yourself up. One, two, three!"

Rosalind pushed up on her foot, and felt herself pulled upward like a sack of potatoes at market. It was not an elegant procedure, but she quickly found herself seated on the branch beside him.

She did not even have time to tuck her skirts beneath her before he took her into his arms and kissed her. She drew in her breath and caught him in her own arms, feeling his solid, reassuring warmth against her.

When his lips released hers, her head fell back and she laughed from sheer exhilaration and utter relief.

"Oh, Michael," she whispered. "I am so glad you are here. When you weren't by the fountain, I feared you had gone to fight Lord Carteret after all."

"I promised you I would not, though I must say it was a difficult promise to keep."

He still held her in his arms, and Rosalind leaned her cheek against his shoulder. It felt so warm, so safe. "I know. I was so very angry with Carteret! I don't think I have ever been so very angry in my life. But Violet is fine now. I was worried about *you*."

"About me? Rosie, there is no need for you to worry about me at all. I am fine, too. More fine than I have ever been before."

Rosalind tilted back her head to stare up at him in the moonlight. Indeed, he did look fine—better than fine. All the anger, the tight rage was gone. He looked young, and happy, and free.

"What has happened?" she asked suspiciously. "An hour ago you could have killed Carteret. Now here you are, happy, sitting in a tree as if you had no cares in the world. What could have happened in that hour?"

"Oh, something very important indeed," he answered lightly. "You see, Rosie, I have learned to follow the rules."

"The rules!" Rosalind was shocked. She did not know *what* she expected him to say, but that—never. "What do you mean? If you intend to become a proper rule-follower now, I am not sure this is the way to go about it. Climbing trees, luring ladies out into the garden alone . . ."

Michael laughed. "Oh, very well, so I will never follow *all* the rules. But I see now why you wrote them."

"Do you indeed?" Rosalind peered closely at him, seeking to see the truth in his eyes. Her rules had been misunderstood by so many people for so long. Never had she wanted someone to understand as much as she wanted *him* to. Yet she scarcely dared to hope. "Truly?"

"Yes. And I know one rule I can happily follow now." He reached inside his coat and drew out a ring, a wondrously beautiful circlet of gold set with a pearl surrounded by small, glittering diamonds. "Mrs. Rosalind Chase, will you do me the great honor of giving me your hand in marriage?"

"What . . . ?" Rosalind gasped. She stared down at the ring in his hand. She feared her mouth was most inelegantly agape, but she could not quite close it. That pearl shone with the glow of the sea in the moonlight, an unearthly, beautiful thing. She had never seen anything like it before. This ring was too beautiful for someone like her.

The man who offered it was too beautiful for someone like her. Yet here he was, holding the ring out to her like some tempting talisman, his angel's face full of hope. She reached one trembling finger out toward the pearl, but could not quite make herself touch it.

"What is that?" she whispered.

Michael laughed nervously. "A betrothal ring, of course. It belonged to my mother, and to my grandmother before her. She always said it would be mine one day, to give to my wife, and since she died it has been kept in the safe in the library here. I fetched it just now—to give it to you. I think you are the only woman in the world who should wear this ring."

Rosalind still felt numb, dumb. She usually considered herself to be a woman of some intelligence, yet she could not string three words together. This was all so unreal, like a dream! Surely she would very soon awaken in her own bed at the Seminary, to find that she had never sat in a tree with a handsome viscount asking her to marry him.

She choked on an hysterical laugh, and pressed her hand to her lips.

Michael appeared so very puzzled and bewildered, as if he was not sure what to make of her reaction or what to say next. He peered down at the ring in his hand. "If you do not care for it, I'm sure I could find something else. A sapphire, or a ruby . . ."

"No!" Rosalind cried. She reached out and folded her hand over his, holding the ring between them. The stones pressed through her thin kid glove into her skin. "It is a beautiful ring, Michael. The most beautiful ring I have ever seen."

"Then it is the suitor you object to?"

"No, of course not."

His face brightened, like dawn breaking over the London grayness, and a smile spread slowly across his lips. "You will marry me, Rosie?"

Her head was spinning. She could not think straight, and that was a terrible thing at this moment, when she was faced with the greatest decision of her life. "Oh, Michael, I just do not know."

"Is it because of that wager? Because of my behavior in the past? I promise you, Rosie, that it is all behind me now." His other hand came up to clasp hers beseechingly and he leaned closer to her. "I am perfectly respectable now. A changed man, I vow!"

Rosalind smiled, and laid her palm against his cheek. The faint prickliness of his evening whiskers tickled through her glove. "Michael, I do not *want* you to be a changed man. You are perfect just as you are. You know that I—care about you."

"Do you care enough to accept me as your husband?"

Oh, yes. If he was a farmer and she was a milkmaid, she would accept him in an instant. But things were so much more complicated than that. "I just do not know, Michael. Everything is so uncertain."

"My feelings for you are *not* uncertain. I love you, Rosie. You are like no other woman I have ever known."

He *loved* her? Rosalind's vision blurred with tears, forcing her to look away from him, to release his hand and brush away the moisture with her fingertips. When had someone last said they loved her? Never. No one had ever said those wonderful words. Not even Charles, or Allen, or her parents. And she had never said it to them. It was as if they were dangerous words, frightening words. Yet they did not scare Michael. He declared his feelings so very openly, to all the world.

It made her dare to be brave, too. Dare to be brave—even though she was shaking in her slippers. "You l-love me?" Her tongue twisted at the word.

"Of course I do. How could I not? You are so beautiful, so very courageous. How many people could run a school as well as you do, *and* write books, *and* look after your brother? And you have done it all by yourself. But I do not want you to be by yourself any longer. I want to be with you, helping you. Please, Rosie, please let me."

Oh, that was so very tempting. To not be all alone, to have someone to walk with her, to make her laugh. To make life into a marvelous adventure, as he always did.

"I just do not know," she said. "I am so confused!"

"Here," he said, reaching for her hand. "Wear the ring for a few days, a week. Look at it, wear it on your finger and think about what I have said." He slid her glove from her arm, her hand, and placed the ring carefully on her finger. The gold band fit perfectly, as if made to go just there. "We can be so happy together, Rosie. Just give me a chance to show you that."

Michael bent his head to press a kiss to her bare fingers. Rosie laid her other hand lightly on his dark curls, felt the silk of them twine over her kid glove.

She knew so very well that he could make her happy. He filled her with such an unimaginable joy just by being near. But could *she* make *him* happy? She knew she was not an exciting woman. She had lived a quiet life, she enjoyed home and hearth and family. He loved her now, but could his poet's heart love her in five, ten years? And his family and circle would judge their match to be a terrible misalliance. He did not care for such things now, yet he very well might later.

It would devastate her to know the warmth of his love, only to lose it later in the chill of regret and contempt.

But still she yearned for him, for that sweet life they could have! A life she had never dared to dream of before.

He raised his head, peering hopefully at her from his beautiful dark eyes. "Will you think about what I have said, Rosie?"

The sensible side of her shouted at her to say no, to turn him away now, to retreat back into her old life. Yet the ring glowed at her, calling to her, whispering that it belonged to her. "Yes," she murmured. "I will think about what you have said, and I will give you my answer very soon."

He gave her an exuberant smile, and swooped down to kiss her hand again. And again. "That is all I can ask—for now."

"I should be going back to the party. I want to look in on Lady Violet again before I leave, and I am sure Georgina will be watching for me."

"Of course. You are right." He slowly, reluctantly let go of her hand, and climbed down from the tree branch. After he had swung to the ground, he reached up to lift her to his side, his clasp warm and secure on her waist. "I doubt anyone will have missed us, though. It has certainly turned into quite an *unusual* party in there."

Oh, yes, Rosalind thought fervently. *A most unusual party indeed.*

And one she would never forget.

"Well. That was certainly not what one expects when one dines out," Georgina exclaimed, as their carriage made its way through the quiet streets back to Wayland House.

Her husband smiled at her, and raised her hand to his lips for a quick kiss. "I would have thought that such raucous goings-on were exactly your cup of tea, Georgie."

Georgina laughed. "Yes, but whoever would have looked for them at Bronston House, of all places!"

"I thought it was terribly amusing," said Lady Emily. "Did you see Lady Islington singing that opera aria? Appalling!" She giggled at the memory.

"If one did not know better, one would suspect Lord Morley of playing a joke on his father," said Georgina. "Those wild young men at his club . . ."

Rosalind, pulled at last from her reverie in the darkened carriage corner, sat straight up and said, "Of course that was not the doing of Mi—Lord Morley! He would never do such a thing."

The thought of someone even *thinking* such a thing, after their tender scene in the garden, sent shooting pains across her brow. She fell back against the leather cushions, her hands pressed to her head.

"Of course he did not, Rosie dear," Georgina said soothingly, worry layered beneath her soft tones. "I was only teasing a bit."

"No one who saw his care for his sister would ever think he would do anything to mar her evening," Emily added gently. "He is a fine gentleman."

"Indeed he is," said Georgina. She leaned forward

to touch Rosalind's hand. "Do you have another head-ache, Rosie? We will be home soon, and my maid can make you one of her tisanes. That always helps me."

"Thank you, Georgie," Rosalind answered weakly. "It is just too many late nights." She could scarcely tell Georgina the true reason for her preoccupation. Not yet.

But Georgina might very well discover it for herself. She paused as her thumb brushed over the ring on Rosalind's finger, hidden beneath the glove.

"Rosie, what is . . . ?" she began. The carriage jolted to a halt in front of Wayland House, and Georgina's husband clasped her arm as the door opened.

"Come, my dear," he said. "You must leave off haranguing poor Mrs. Chase now. We are home."

"Haranguing?" Georgina protested loudly, as she stepped out into the night. "I was not *haranguing* any-one, I was merely asking . . ."

Her voice faded as she went up the stairs and disap-peared through the front door, her husband and sister-in-law behind her.

Rosalind sat by herself for a moment in the aban-doned carriage, filling her lungs with air and silence. This was the first time she had been truly alone all evening—but it did not help to clear her head. She was just as confused as ever.

"Ma'am?" the footman said softly, as he offered his white-gloved hand to help her alight.

There was nothing to do now but go upstairs and go to bed. Surely she would feel better in the morning.

She stepped down from the carriage and followed the others into the house. In the foyer, she found that, blessedly, Georgina had already retired. Only a maid waited to take Rosalind's wrap, and the butler with a letter on his silver tray.

"This came for you while you were out, Mrs. Chase," he said, holding out the tray. "I thought it might be of some urgency."

"Thank you," Rosalind said. She picked up the mis-sive with a pang of trepidation. Letters waiting at night could not be good. Was this from that banker again? The handwriting was not familiar, the stationery plain white vellum.

She broke the wax wafer and read quickly.

"Not bad news, I trust, Mrs. Chase," the butler said.

Rosalind looked up at him with a smile. "Not at all. It is from my publisher. He wishes to see me tomorrow morning."

The butler appeared a bit puzzled at the mention of a publisher, but he was so well-trained that his expression quickly cleared to blandness. "Very good, ma'am. Shall I order the carriage to be brought around for you in the morning?"

"Yes, thank you. About ten o'clock, I think. Good night."

"Good night, ma'am."

Rosalind went upstairs, her letter folded in her ring-bedecked hand. Well, at least one thing was looking more positive now. Her headache had even eased. Tomorrow, all would be made clear.

Chapter Nineteen

"The home and family are the lady's sphere—
she must protect them at all costs."
—*A Lady's Rules for Proper Behavior*, Chapter One

Rosalind stepped out the door of her publisher's office into the late morning sunshine, her step lighter than it had been in days, if not months. She even hummed a lilting little waltz tune under her breath as she took the footman's hand and stepped into Georgina's waiting carriage.

This was truly a lovely day, she thought, as she watched the scenery roll past outside the open landau. The air was warm, the light bright, and London really far more interesting than she had once thought it. The shop windows held an infinite array of enticing goods—fabrics in vibrant colors and gentle pastels, books in rich leather bindings, slippers, parasols, bonnets. And the people—the people all appeared so very agreeable. Rosalind sat back against the carriage cushions with a happy sigh.

Of course, what made this day so very fine was the news that her publisher wanted a new volume from her as quickly as possible. A guidebook specifically for young ladies about to make their come-outs. It was precisely the sort of thing she truly wanted to write. Perhaps it would prevent any other unsuspecting girls from facing what poor Violet had last night.

Rosalind shifted her reticule in her palm, listening to the clink of coins inside. She had even managed to talk the publisher into giving her an advance on the new volume's profits—enough to pay off most of Allen's loan.

But the coins were not even the best part of the day, as lovely as they were. The very best part resided on her finger, hidden beneath her glove.

Under the cover of a fold of her dark green pelisse, Rosalind drew off the glove and stared down at that ring. Last night, in the moonlight, it had glowed with a mellow promise. Today, the diamonds encircling the pearl caught the sun and reflected it back to her radiantly. Just like the sparkle of Michael's own personality.

"Oh, Michael," she whispered. "What am I to do? What *should* I do?"

The ring glinted in mute answer. Rosalind had stayed awake almost all the night, thinking, thinking. Every fiber of her sensible self told her that such a match could never work. Her mind urged her to go back to her school, and forget about such a life, forget about *him*. Especially since she had this new book to work on.

But her heart—ah, her heart cried out something very different. It told her to grab this man and run with him to Gretna Green immediately! It wanted more poetry, more nighttime tree climbing, more waltzes, more kisses, more—more *everything*. She had always been able to silence her heart in the past, to bury it beneath prudence and good sense. Now, it would not quiet.

"I deserve happiness," she told herself. "I deserve something for myself after all this time."

But did she truly?

The carriage lurched to a halt, caught in one of the London traffic snarls. Up ahead, a wagon was overturned, blocking everyone else from moving. Rosalind pulled her glove back over the ring, and glanced about at the people near her.

A few carriages over sat Lady Clarke, with a handsome blond gentleman Rosalind had never seen before. As she watched, Lady Clarke noticed her, and tugged at her companion's arm. She whispered in his ear, and gestured toward Rosalind. The man laughed, giving Rosalind an insolent stare.

Her cheeks burning, Rosalind turned quickly away and stared resolutely ahead. She had known, of course, that people would be bound to talk once she had been seen in public—several times!—with the famous Viscount Morley. And she had expected it to sting. After all, she had spent all of her life being a pattern card of propriety. But, somehow, the embarrassment was not nearly as grave as she would once have thought it.

It seemed a small price to pay for all she had experienced here with Michael. Yet would she think that still if she went back to her school to find no pupils to return to?

If you were Michael's wife, it would not matter, her heart whispered temptingly.

The carriage moved on once more, turning down the street toward Wayland House. She had no time to worry about such things now. Georgina and Emily would be waiting; after luncheon, they were meant to go on a shopping expedition. Rosalind actually had her eye on a bolt of sapphire-colored satin at a certain warehouse, the first expensive fabric she had thought of for herself in years.

It would make up a fine wedding gown, that subversive voice in her heart said.

"Enough!" Rosalind exclaimed aloud.

"Ma'am?" the footman who had come to assist her from the carriage asked, obviously surprised. "Did you ask something?"

"Oh, no, not at all." Her cheeks warm yet again, she took his hand and stepped down onto the pavement. The butler opened the front door, anticipating her arrival, but as Rosalind turned to go up the walkway, something caught her attention. She whirled about to see that man again—the one she had seen at least twice before, lurking outside Wayland House.

He lounged against the iron fence of the park across the way, his face twisted away from her, but she *knew* this was the same man.

He could not possibly have any business there! Perhaps he was from the bank. Or—or something worse.

"Ma'am?" the footman asked. "Is something amiss?"

"No," Rosalind muttered. "Not at all, thank you." She whirled around and walked as quickly as she could without racing to the front door.

Georgina was crossing the foyer to the drawing room, a paint box in her hand, but she stopped in her tracks when Rosalind slammed the door and leaned back against the heavy wood. "Rosie? What is wrong? Is a ghost chasing you? Was it bad news at your publisher?"

Rosalind shook her head. She could not speak; she could scarcely breathe. She did not know what was happening, but a cold knot twisted in her stomach. "That man is back," she managed to croak out.

Georgina's brow creased. "What man?"

Rosalind had forgotten that she had not told anyone about the lurker. She had thought she was imagining things, until today. "I have seen this man standing across the street a few times. I thought surely I was hallucinating, yet there he is again today. Oh, Georgie, I do not like this at all!"

Georgina'a eyes caught green fire—not a good sign. "As well you should not! You should have told me earlier, Rosie. *No one* spies on *my* house and gets away with it! Come with me. We will soon discover what this is all about."

Before Rosalind could even catch a breath, Georgina shoved her box into the butler's hands and caught up a walking stick from the stand. She threw open the front door and hurried down the walkway. As Rosalind followed, Georgina yanked the stick apart, revealing a hidden sword.

"Which one?" Georgina asked, in a hard voice Rosalind had never heard from her before.

Rosalind pointed mutely. Georgina stormed across the street, and before the spy could even suspect the storm that approached him, she had the tip of the sword pressed to his throat.

"Who are you and why are you spying on my house?" she demanded.

The man, who had appeared so very insolent and indolent only a moment before, gulped and turned a most unattractive pea green shade. He held his hands up in apparent surrender.

"I am not *spying* on anyone's house," he gasped. "I am merely out enjoying the fine weather."

"My friend tells me you have been 'enjoying the weather' here several times." Georgina pressed the blade closer. Rosalind felt scared out of her wits, yet she could not help but admire that iron resolve—and wish for some of it herself.

"I do not know what you're talking about. I simply like this park," the man said. "And *you*, madam, are attracting a great deal of attention. I suggest you put the blade down before you are arrested."

Rosalind glanced about. They were indeed gathering a gawking crowd. Georgina just laughed. "Do you know who I am? I am the Duchess of Wayland. No one will arrest me, even if I spit you like a wild boar right here. You are obviously a vile kidnapper, and my children are walking with their nanny in this very park. No one would fault me for defending my family."

"Now, just a moment—" the man began, but he was cut off when Georgina pressed the blade closer.

A man on horseback came galloping up the street, and the crowd parted to let him through. The Duke of Wayland swung down from his horse and strode through the crowd, looking neither to the right nor left, just straight at his wife.

"Georgina," he said, quietly but firmly. "What has happened now?"

"I am very glad you are here, darling," Georgina said, her sword never wavering. "Rosalind has seen this man spying on our house. He is obviously scheming to kidnap Elizabeth Anne and Sebastian."

"Indeed?" Alex stepped closer and removed the sword from his wife's hand, his dark, handsome face like implacable granite.

"No!" the man cried out, his upheld hands shaking. "I am no kidnapper. I was merely paid to watch this house."

"Paid to track my children's movements?" the duke demanded.

"It had nothing to do with your family at all, Y-Your Grace!"

"Then why are you spying on my house?"

"I was paid to watch *her*!" The man pointed a trembling finger at Rosalind.

"Me?" Rosalind whispered. Everyone swung about to stare at her.

Everyone but Alex, whose gaze never wavered from the villain's face. "That is just as bad. Mrs. Chase is a guest in my home. Who wants her followed? Speak quickly, and I may allow you to live."

The man turned even more green. "It was the Earl of Athley! He paid me. I have been following her for weeks, even before she came to London."

The Earl of Athley? Michael's father? Rosalind pressed her hand to her mouth.

Georgina laid a comforting hand on her arm. "Oh, Rosie," she murmured. "The Earl of Athley. Such a terrible potential father-in-law. It is just fortunate that his son is so very attractive. He must take after his mother."

Attractive. Yes, indeed. Michael was that.

But was he attractive enough? Rosalind thought that now, at last, she knew the answer to that question.

Chapter Twenty

"A young lady's most important decision is who she will marry—she must choose with her head, not her heart."
—*A Lady's Rules for Proper Behavior,* Chapter Ten

Michael handed his hat and walking stick to the butler at Bronston House, glancing about the foyer as he did so. The place was as gloomy as ever, dark, hulking furniture pushed back into place, dust motes dancing in the narrow bars of sunlight falling from between the velvet draperies. There were no signs of the previous night's unexpectedly raucous soiree.

That could almost have been a dream, a product of fairy spells and full moons. An aberration in the atmosphere. Yet he knew it could not be. His time with Rosalind in the garden, nestled on the wide tree branch, had felt so real. The sight of his mother's ring on her elegant finger, the diamondlike tears in her eyes—all wonderfully real. He never could have dreamed it.

Strange. He had always imagined that he would be nervous when he asked a lady to marry him, would be loathe to give up his freedom for duty. He had been as calm and steady as he had ever been when he took Rosalind's hand and asked her to be his wife, *more* steady even. He had not been loathe to give up anything—only excited to be gaining something infinitely precious.

It was right. It was meant to be. He could only pray that Rosalind felt the same way, for he had had no word from her yet today. But her kiss had not lied. She loved him, as he loved her. And he would do anything to make her see that.

"Is my sister downstairs yet?" Michael asked the butler. Hopefully, Violet would be in her little sitting room, and he could slip in there to see her without alerting their father to his presence. He had no desire to deal with the irascible earl, today of all days.

"Not quite yet, my lord, though her maid just took Lady Violet's chocolate up to her. She should be down very soon. But Lord Athley is in the drawing room and wishes to see you, my lord."

Damn and blast. "I suppose he knows I am here, then?"

"Oh, yes, my lord. He saw your carriage from the window." The butler bowed, and strode briskly away with Michael's hat and stick.

Well, it seemed he was well and truly trapped. He had to see for himself that Violet was unscathed by her ordeal last night, and in order to do that he had to stay at Bronston House.

"Ah, well," he muttered. "Might as well get it over with."

He went into the drawing room and closed the doors firmly behind him. In here, too, the signs of the night's ravages were few. Aside from some drooping roses left in the vases, everything was back to its normal aspect. The draperies were drawn, and, despite the warmth of the spring day, a fire blazed in the hearth, casting an ominous glow on the carved stone crest.

The earl sat in a high-backed, thronelike chair before that fire, a woolen shawl wrapped about his shoulders, his gouty leg propped on a footstool. He looked up sullenly with bloodshot eyes as Michael crossed the room to sit on one of the settees set a bit farther away from the flames' heat.

"I told your foolish aunt I would rue the day I allowed her and your bloodless sister to have a rout here!" the earl grumbled without preamble. "I knew it was a poor idea. Company brings nothing but trouble, trouble and mess. There is no one left in London worth knowing. It is just parvenus and mushrooms. And *now* see what has happened!"

Had Violet told their father what had happened in the conservatory? Michael cursed silently. She had been so agitated, but he should have warned her about saying anything to the earl. "If you are referring to Lord Carteret's reprehensible behavior . . ."

"Carteret?" the earl shouted. "Was it that insolent puppy who did it? By God, but I will send the Bow Street Runners after him to get it back! That dirty thief."

"Thief?" Michael frowned in confusion. A cad Carteret undoubtedly was, but a thief? "What was taken?"

"Someone broke into the library safe last night and stole your mother's pearl ring. There is no telling what else is missing in the house. If it was that Carteret . . ."

Michael burst into surprised laughter. His father actually thought a thief had been in the safe! This was absurd. The man was becoming bacon-brained in his dotage—not that he had ever exactly been a clear thinker.

The earl scowled, and swiped out with his walking stick. Michael was too far away for the blow to do anything more than stir the hot air about.

"You young idiot!" he growled. "What are you laughing at? A crime has been committed!"

"I hardly think so, Father. Mother left her ring to me, and I am the one who took it. There was no thievery involved."

The earl turned a most unattractive shade of purple. "*You* took the ring?"

"Yes. Did you not wonder why nothing else in the safe was missing? Mother's sapphires are there, not to mention her diamond tiara and a great amount of coin."

"You had no right to just take that ring! What did you want it for? To sell it for gambling money?"

"Of course not. I wanted it for the purpose Mother intended it for—to give it to the lady I mean to marry."

The earl's face cleared a bit, and he leaned forward in his chair. This was a theme he had been harping on for years, Michael's duty to wed and produce a new little heir. "Indeed? Well, why did you not say so! It is about time you did your duty. Who is it? Miss Sanderson? Lady Eveline Ferry?"

"It is Mrs. Rosalind Chase," Michael said calmly. "I am sure you will wish us happy."

That purple color suffused the earl's cheeks again, and for a moment Michael feared he might have apoplexy right here and now. He rose from his chair to fetch a brandy, but was driven back a step when his father's thrown stick hit him square in the chest.

"How dare you!" the earl shouted. "You have always been willfully blind to your duty, but this is too much even for you. Marrying a schoolmistress, a red-haired adventuress . . ."

Michael had heard more than enough. He snapped the stick in two with his bare hands and threw the jagged halves into the fire. "You will not speak of my future wife in such a manner."

"Your *wife*! A woman older than you, with no fortune, no family, a brother who gambles away what little money they have? A woman who has business with *bankers*? I know all of this and more, Michael, because I knew you and your stupid sister were caught in that woman's snare. That your sister was far too attached to her and that school. So I hired a man to follow her, even before she came here to London to entrap you."

The earl sat back in his chair, oozing with a smug satisfaction. Michael suddenly wished he had not thrown that stick into the fire so precipitously, so he could beat his father over the head with it now. How *dare* that monster set a spy to follow Rosie!

"If you thought this news would dissuade me from marrying Mrs. Chase, you were much mistaken," he said, in a low, tight voice. "I love her, and I am more resolved than ever to make her my wife. And now, I bid you farewell."

He spun on his heel and strode out of the room, before he gave in to his overwhelming desire to commit murder. He ignored the earl's shouts, and closed the doors behind him.

Violet stood halfway down the staircase, her hands clutched on the balustrade. Her face was a bit pale from her adventures of the night before, but a brilliant smile curved her lips and her eyes sparkled. She did not even seem to hear the screams and thumps from the drawing room, as she ran down the stairs to throw her arms about Michael.

"Oh, my darling brother!" she cried. "Are you truly going to marry Mrs. Chase?"

"If she will have me."

"Of course she will have you! She *must*. You are the finest catch in London, Michael, and this is the best decision you have ever made. To think—she will be my *sister*. Oh, Michael. Last night was the worst night of my life, but this is the very best day."

China shattered behind the drawing room door. Michael gave Violet a rueful smile. "As you can tell, Vi, Father is not wildly happy about my choice of bride."

Violet cast a hard glance at the door. Her look was strangely contemptuous—an expression Michael had never seen on his sister's sweet face. It was as if she had grown up in only a day. "Who cares about him? He can do nothing to you. Mrs. Chase will one day be the finest countess this house has ever seen, after Mother, of course. And *I* will dance with the greatest of joy at your wedding!"

Michael laughed. He twirled her to him and gave her a resounding kiss on both cheeks. "Vi, you are the very best of sisters! And I promise that you *shall* dance at my wedding. Now, I want you to get out of this house, go call on Aunt Minnie for the afternoon. Mrs. Chase and I will come see you later."

"What a fine idea. Aunt Minnie did have a new bonnet she wanted to show me."

Michael kissed Violet's cheek again, and framed her face in his hands as he examined her closely. "Are you truly well today, Vi?"

She clasped his hands in hers and gave him a reassuring smile. "I am fine. Never better, now that I have heard your news. Really, there was no harm done. I was saved by the rules, you know."

Michael laughed again. "My dearest sister, I think we both were."

Chapter Twenty-one

> "Always marry a gentleman whose character and background you are sure of. This is the only assurance for future happiness."
> —*A Lady's Rules for Proper Behavior*, Chapter Two

"*W*hat a truly extraordinary day," Georgina said, leaning back in her chair with a deep sigh. She swirled a crystal goblet of restorative brandy between her hands. "I vow, Rosie, you must have dragged all the excitement behind you from the country. Town was deadly dull until you arrived, and now look at all that has happened!"

Rosalind laughed, and sipped at her own brandy. Its warm sharpness was comforting. She had been more shaken by the encounter with Lord Athley's spy than she cared to admit. "I do believe it was *you* who created most of the excitement today, Georgie, drawing a sword on the man like that. You seemed like a lady pirate from a hundred years ago."

Georgina shrugged. "I am rather sensitive about people threatening my family and friends—even people who are so unsubtle in their spying that it is all rather a joke."

"Indeed. I do hope Lord Athley was not paying him a great deal. Or perhaps he could get his money back?"

Georgina snickered. "Oh, Rosie, you made a joke! You must be feeling better."

"I am feeling quite well, thank you." And, strangely enough, she was. The shock of discovering that Michael's father had set a spy on her—on *her,* the dullest woman in Town!—had faded. She felt only a still, centered calm, and an odd urge to fall on the floor laughing.

"That is good. Everyone knows that Lord Athley is truly a cranky old eccentric, but this goes beyond that. It is worthy of Bedlam." Georgina drank the last of her brandy and put the glass down on the table beside her. "I do hope that this incident will not affect your good opinion of Lord Morley, Rosie. He is a good man, and he does seem to care about you so much."

Rosalind smiled at her serenely. "Of course not. Lord Morley is not liable for his father's faults. He is entirely his own man." Indeed, Rosalind had come to a decision concerning Michael and herself before she even discovered the truth about the spy. Seeing how truly pitiful his father was had only increased her resolve. She knew truly that she had made the right decision, and she would not be swayed from it.

"I am surprised that Lord Morley and Lady Violet are the offspring of that lunatic at all," Georgina mused. "They are both so very charming."

"Perhaps their mother had a *chere ami,*" Rosalind suggested. "At least I hope the poor lady did. I am sure she deserved some happiness in her life."

Georgina stared at her, wide-eyed. "Rosie? Do you have a fever? You do not sound at all like yourself today."

"Do I not?" Rosalind tilted her head, considering this. "Funny. For I feel more like myself than I ever have before."

Georgina shook her head, obviously perplexed. "You should go to bed for the rest of the day. I am sure a rest would do you good."

"I am not a bit tired."

"Then have some more brandy." Georgina leaned across the table to pour more of the amber liquid into both of their glasses.

As Rosalind took a small sip, there was a quick knock at the drawing room door. "Lord Morley is here to see Mrs. Chase, Your Grace," the butler announced.

"Ah, yes, right on time. I do like a man who has a sense of timing," said Georgina. "Show him in."

Rosalind sat straight up in her chair, a nervous excitement that had nothing to do with the liquor dancing up her spine. She reached up to pat at her hair, and pushed stray curls back into their pins.

"I see that is my cue to depart," Georgina said. She stood and gathered her silk shawl about her as Michael came into the room. "Lord Morley, how lovely to see you again. You must excuse me, as I promised my daughter I would read to her before her nap. But Mrs. Chase would certainly enjoy a nice long chat with you." With that, she breezed from the room, shutting the door firmly behind her.

Rosalind hoped she was not listening at the keyhole. She smiled a bit at the image of her elegant friend kneeling on the floor, straining to spy on them, as she stood and held her hands out to Michael.

He was certainly every bit as handsome as he always was, with his dark hair tousled by the wind and an emerald twinkling from the folds of his mint green cravat. Yet there was an agitation about him, a nervous energy that fairly crackled in the air around him. He took her hands tightly in his, but did not raise them to his lips. They just stood there in the middle of the room, hands clasped, like figures in a *tableau vivant*.

Rosalind herself felt oddly unable to move, or talk, or even breathe. She had rehearsed so carefully in her mind what she wanted to say when this moment came. That was gone now; she remembered not a syllable. She saw only him. He alone filled all her mind.

What would the rule be? she asked herself. She had no idea. She could scarcely even remember what a *rule* was.

"Is that true? Would you enjoy a—chat with me?" he asked thickly.

"I—well, yes, I suppose. I did hope you might call at some point today."

"I wanted to come at the break of daylight! Oh, Rosie, there were so many things I wanted to say to you. I could have written an epic! Now I find that I must begin with this—I apologize."

Rosalind opened her mouth, all set to answer him— and she tripped over her tongue. That was *not* the question she was about to reply to! "You apologize? Michael, whatever for? Are you . . ." A chill settled an icy grasp around her heart. "Are you withdrawing your offer to me?"

"What!" His clasp tightened convulsively. "Never, Rosie. You shall not escape from me as easily as that. I saw my father this morning, and he told me something so abominable, so evil, I could not credit it even from him."

"Did he tell you about the man he paid to follow me?"

"Yes. But how did you know?" Michael's face darkened. "Did the bast—the earl come here? Did he threaten you?"

Rosalind laughed. "No, indeed! In fact, Georgina drew a sword on the poor hired spy and threatened to, er, 'spit him like a wild boar.' Your father was obviously too cheap to pay for a true master spy, because the man acknowledged the whole scheme to us at once." She laughed again, at the memory of his terrified expression when Georgina brandished her blade.

Michael laughed, too, though it was decidedly bitter. "And you were not angry at all?"

"Of course I was angry. No one likes to be followed about, and for him to involve Georgina and her family was truly infuriating. Yet it helped me to see something even more clearly."

"Oh? And what is that?"

Rosalind smiled up at him. "That I love you and want to spend my life with you. That you could become the man you are—so openhearted, and kind, and funny—after growing up with such a father is nothing less than a wonder."

Michael threw back his head and laughed, and this time there was no trace of bitterness. There was only a pure, crystalline joy. "Say it again!" he demanded.

Rosalind giggled. "What part?"

"The part where you said you love me."

"I love you! I adore you. And I will marry you, before you come to your senses and see what a poor choice you have made."

"I have made the best choice, for I am marrying the most beautiful woman in England, and the most clever and the bravest." Michael sat down on the nearest chair and pulled her onto his lap.

Once she would have been truly appalled. This was a most blatant violation of the rules! A lady should never behave like a tavern maid, especially not in a ducal drawing room. Now she giggled like a schoolgirl, and twined her arms about his neck. "The bravest?"

"Most ladies after meeting my father would run the other way," he answered, nuzzling a kiss against her throat. "Not you, my redheaded Valkyrie. My beautiful defender."

"Then it would seem we are well and truly betrothed," Rosalind said, with a happy sigh. All her doubts, her old weaknesses, were fallen away. This was the right thing to do—this was her future.

Michael took her hand and pressed his lips to her palm. He turned it over—and paused. "If we are truly betrothed, my Rosie, then where is your ring? Never say my father's spy stole it from you!"

"Of course not." Rosalind reached up into the tight long sleeve of her gown and pulled out the ring. She placed it in his hand. "It is silly, but I just wanted you to put it on my finger again, now that there is no doubt about either of our feelings."

He grinned at her. "Very well. Mrs. Rosalind Chase, will you marry me?"

"Viscount Morley, I will."

Michael slid the ring back onto her finger, where it dazzled in the sunlight from the tall windows. He lifted her hand and kissed it lingeringly, moving his lips over her fingers. "You are truly mine now."

Rosalind leaned her cheek against the silk of his hair. "As you are mine?"

He stared up at her intently. "I am always and forever yours, Rosie. When will you marry me? Tomorrow?"

"Tomorrow!"

"I am sure I could procure a special license. Perhaps the Waylands would let us have the wedding here?"

Rosalind was quite sure Georgina would be delighted to have the wedding here, and would immediately launch into arrangements. It was a good thing Georgina's taste was so excellent, for Rosalind's own head was spinning far too much to think of licenses and flowers and cake. "It is all so sudden . . ."

"Or we could make a dash for Gretna Green! Anything you want, Rosie. Anything—if you will only marry me. But I know you have arrangements you'll need to make."

"So I do. I have already written to Miss James, one of my teachers. She is a very competent young lady, and I am sure she will be able to look after the Seminary for the next term. I only have to let Allen know, so he can be here for the wedding."

"Next week, then," Michael said eagerly. "And not a day later! We will wed here, and then I am taking you to Italy."

Rosalind gasped. "Italy!"

"I trust there are no objections? If there is someplace else you would rather go . . ."

"Oh, no. I have always dreamed of seeing Italy. Georgina says that Venice is the most romantic place in the world. It is so full of history, so warm and sunny."

"So far from my father."

"Indeed. Another great advantage of Italy. I have no objections at all. Perhaps Violet would care to join us? Travel can be so educational."

"You *are* an extraordinary lady, my Rosie. Not many women would want their sister-in-law along on their wedding trip."

"Violet is a dear. I cannot see that she would give us any trouble, unless she falls in love with some dark-eyed Italian. And Italy *is* very far from your father. I am sure it would vex him greatly to have us all so far out of his reach."

Michael gave a whoop of laughter, and kissed her again and again. And yet again, longer and sweeter. "You *are* a sly one. In fact, I am sure such deviousness must be against the rules," he murmured, when he at last raised his lips from hers.

Rosalind leaned back against his shoulder and sighed happily. "Ah, but my darling Michael, I have discovered that there is really only one rule that should never be broken."

He nuzzled her cheek, blowing lightly on the loose curls at her temple. "And what rule is that?"

"The rule of true love, of course."

Signet Regency Romance from

Amanda McCabe

**Available wherever books are sold or
to order call 1-800-788-6262**

S057

Allison Lane

"A FORMIDABLE TALENT...
MS. LANE NEVER FAILS TO
DELIVER THE GOODS."
—*ROMANTIC TIMES*

Emily's Beau

0-451-20992-3

Emily Hughes has her sights set on one man:
Jacob Winters, Earl of Hawthorne. But her
hopes are dashed when she discovers that Jacob
is already betrothed. She will have to forget
Jacob and marry another, which is just what
she plans to do—until one moonlit kiss changes
everything.

Also Available:

Birds of a Feather	0-451-19825-5
The Purloined Papers	0-451-20604-5
Kindred Spirits	0-451-20743-2

Available wherever books are sold, or
to order call: 1-800-788-6262